THE SECRET OF ETERNAL YOUTH

Margaret Swift

THE SECRET OF ETERNAL YOUTH

Margaret Swift

Happy Reading!

Margaret Swift

THE SECRET OF ETERNAL YOUTH
by Margaret Swift
Copyright © Margaret Swift 2007

First published 2007
by Cockasnook Books,
22 Whernside Road, Nottingham, NG5 4LD
www.cockasnook.co.uk

Printed by The Russell Press,
Russell House, Bulwell Lane, Basford, Nottingham NG6 0BT

Reprinted 2009

ISBN 978-0-9557460-1-7

Cover illustration by Lesley Lawrence

"I sincerely love and worship trees and know that they are people"

Paul Nash

Torquella

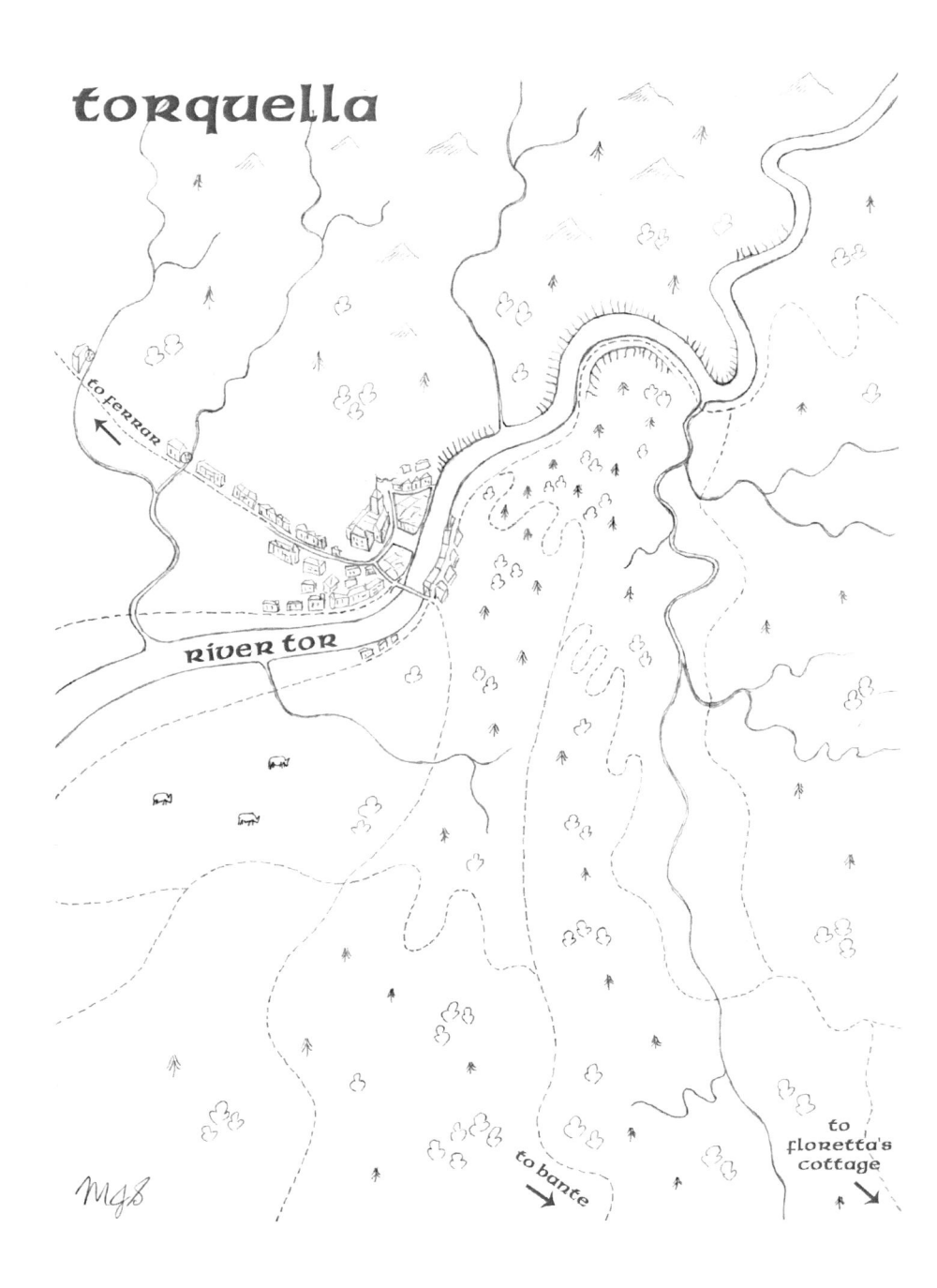

PROLOGUE

Night was already drawing in when, against her mother's opposition, she took her heavy cloak from the wooden peg beside the doorway and wrapped it about her slender form, covering the rich glow of her red-gold hair with the dark hood and pulling the thick folds so tight about her that her loveliness was scarce apparent. This young woman was a creature of great beauty; hence her mother's concern for her. For, although the part of the forest where they lived was deserted and lonely, if she persisted in going out so often and in wandering so far, surely one day she would stray into the path of an unscrupulous and lecherous vagabond. At that time of year, he would not have been so readily aware of the perfection of her physical form, her heavy cloak concealing her loveliness so considerably, but then, the time of year provided far more immediate dangers: it was winter.

With a parting word and a glance at her slumbering babe, she left the warmth of the tightly shuttered cottage; shunned its cosy hearth for the bleakness of a sunless forest twilight. She saw that winter had already gained a firm hold; no snow had yet fallen but there was a bitter cold gripping the forest, gripping the very air, which promised snow. The forest remained without life or movement, as if all the tiny forest creatures – birds, squirrels and insects – had hidden themselves away in anticipation of a storm and as though even the trees were stilled in expectation.

All was dim; not a single ray of sunshine reached down through the bare black branches; indeed, the branches were locked together in a frozen haze, opaque and hard as ice, through which the distant winter sun could not hope to warm itself a path. All was sombre; a sadness pervaded the forest, a melancholy, which began to touch at the heart of the young woman as her dark cloaked figure picked its way through the gloom, over rocks and mosses, over stiff frozen leaves and brittle crackling twigs.

Apart from her footfall, everything was perfectly quiet; there was no breath of wind, no hint of movement, nowhere among the bushes nor even in the highest branches of the trees. The forest was muted, hushed, as if in mourning. All life appeared suspended, even the bright leaves and berries of the evergreen bushes were frozen to a crystallised lifelessness, like so many delicate and expensive fruits candied for a king to eat.

As she walked on, the biting cold began to gnaw at her tender flesh, even through the long thick folds of her felty cloak. She shivered as her fingers and toes began to freeze, yet she did not turn back to the sanctuary of her cottage. Instead, she headed directly away from it into a part of the forest where the trees grew thickest and where human foot rarely trod.

So glad was she to be out of doors after the succession of household chores which had confined her all day that she could feel almost oblivious to the cold. Instead of complaining to herself about her blue fingernails or bewailing the thin, roughly cobbled soles of her boots, she breathed in the chill air deeply and sighed with relief. Walking alone in the deepest parts of the forest was her chief source of pleasure and relaxation, her greatest joy.

She thought to herself, "It is fortunate that I come today, for the forest is so sad. The winter is harsh this year and the trees are suffering. Now that I have come, I can offer them consolation and try to brighten this dark day for them. I have come all too rarely recently. Maybe that is why the trees are so sad and the forest so still. I have neglected them; I failed to come when they were most in need of a loving gesture…"

She wandered on in the eerie half-light of the forest and then, suddenly, a soft breeze blew and there came a whispering in the trees. "We are silent because we fear for you. Go home, loved one. This cold is more than your human blood can bear."

"Have no fear," came the soft tones of her gentle reply. "You need not feel concerned for me. When I am with you and among you, my heart feels only warmth and then I am home."

"So you say, loved one, but we fear you hide your discomfort from us, you deceive us, you deceive yourself. You are brave, but you are too brave. You must turn back, must turn back…"

"In a short while I will turn," she replied. "When I hear a cheer in your words, when I have dispelled the feeling of gloom which is cast over you."

"No! Turn now, now, before it is too late! Unless you return home now there can be no cheer in our words today."

"Not yet," she insisted. "In your selflessness you seek to deprive yourself of me. I will not allow you to do this. I know that you prefer to have me with you. And I know that you will always protect me."

"For once we are powerless to protect you if you will not heed our warning." The breeze in the branches became stronger as the tone of the forest grew more pressing: "Though it is clear to us that you will not listen, still we implore you! Turn back! Turn back! Now!"

Even as the voice of the forest reached its most shrill, a sudden wind arose and a capricious gust caught at the young woman's hood and snatched it rudely back, baring her soft face to the keenness of the wind. Her hair was whipped about and slapped across her face, into her mouth so that she gasped and into her eyes so that they stung. She became gradually aware that the forest was still attempting to speak to her but she could no longer hear the words for the howling of the wind; she could catch merely the urgency of them.

"So the warning is in earnest," she thought, "and I must go home. This wind is an omen, contrived by the trees to encourage me towards greater caution…"

So she turned about at last, facing into the wind now and heading for home, pulling her hood close around her face once more, eyes half closed, more feeling the way by the direction of the wind than following any path she knew. Believing the gale to be the forest's creation, she expected it soon to abate now that she was heeding its timely warning, but even as she took her first paces towards home, she was to realise her misunderstanding, for instead, the wind blew still harder, tearing at her clothes and penetrating into her face and flesh with needles of ice so that she could now scarcely bear to open her eyes.

Now the wind chose to blow from all sides: it would appear at first almost to be helping her along, and then it would hesitate, fluctuate and decide instead to confront her, pinning her back from homeward movement with a great invisible force. It would then relent so that she stumbled with the impetus of her forward effort and would blow instead upwards, lifting her skirts about her almost humorously so that she nearly left the ground. Then it would beat downwards onto her in harsh heavy gusts, flattening her hood against her head and face so that she caught her breath.

As she attempted to open her eyes to find her way, she realised suddenly that she could not; neither could she feel her way by the wind now, its direction having grown changeable, and she feared that by following the wind, she might already have erred from her path. She comforted herself with the thought that the forest would surely direct her, but then, she wondered, how could it? How could the trees make any message clear above the awful howling of this wind? They could not.

She had only her own resources, for neither could the trees use their branches to prompt and guide her: they could not compete with the force of this terrible storm.

Even as she became aware of the true danger of her situation, she felt on her cheeks the promise of further peril. She noticed with surprise that her face had become wet, but not with a heavy wetness as of rain; the moisture was soft and dewy. The touch of it upon her cheek was gentle and she recognised it as the touch of falling snow. She felt at first glad, for she normally welcomed the onset of the snow, the beautiful snows… the lovely snows which lent the forest a deep ermine mantle… She welcomed them, even though they would confine her to the area of her cottage for weeks.

With her next breath she realised the harsh fact of the additional danger and her temporary elation left her. Strangely, this elation was not replaced by fear: she felt weak now and from the weakness came a soothing drowsiness. She stood still, feeling as if she were not there, amid the great billows of snow, snow and more snow, descending at unaccustomed speed from the heavily burdened sky. She could feel it blowing everywhere about her now, seeking each fold of clothing, each crevice of skin, a feathery caress upon flesh now almost unfeeling, now numb to the cold. Standing there with her eyes closed she grew aware of a curious absence of fear; she was aware only that she should feel fear.

With this awareness came a last spur to action. She began to move forward again. Step by step, she fought her way through the storm, concentrating on maintaining a straight path in the direction she felt was home, head down now and gripping her cloak grimly about her in opposition to the merciless wind which sought to rip it from her. Once more the wind succeeded in tearing back her hood, wrapping her hair about her face so tightly that her hands moved instinctively to free her eyes. She drew her hair back with near frozen fingers, her face into the wind, and in this instant the wind whipped craftily at her cloak, snapping the strong cords which secured it as if they were single threads. The cloak billowed out like a sail on a boat and left her, rising high with the wind, ever upwards, dancing here and there between the branches of the trees. For a moment she span about snatching blindly and with unfeeling hands to retrieve it.

And then she was glad it was gone. For, without it, her body had become pure ice so that she would feel no more physical pain. She was no longer constrained by the need to grip her cloak feebly about herself; she was no longer forced to shiver or to blink. Her spirit was liberated and relinquished human form and became one with the forest and soared ecstatically high through the trees. In this same instant her body stumbled and fell, finding a comfortable and fitting place to lie in a little hollow, sheltered from the wind and protected by the exposed roots of an ancient oak, so that her frozen form could become one with the snows which sought eagerly to combine with her and so that she could sink forever into the rich soils beneath. This was peace. But for the forest that day there was no peace; the wind howled still and with it moaned ever louder and every more distraught the voice of the mourning forest.

CHAPTER 1

Upon a soft mossy bank in a secluded glade, a young girl was sleeping, intoxicated by the drowsy warmth of a strong summer sun. She lay completely relaxed but gave no impression of languidness, for a vitality and joy in living distinguished her even in sleep; stretched out, but neither slumped nor sprawled, for her delightful form was possessed of a prevalent grace. Her features too retained their dignity as she slumbered: no looseness of line nor lowness of mentality marked her countenance. Most striking was her long thick hair: not restrained into some orderly style nor draped about her shoulders, it issued spiritedly in all directions about her head, rather as a child might depict the rays of the sun. Yet its appearance denied any charge of untidiness: such was the symmetry of the pattern which her locks unconsciously assumed that they might well have been arranged so.

She slept on; the play of sunbeams upon her upturned face could not rouse her. But her inactivity called for no accusation of indolence: this rest was well deserved. In recent months the increasing disability of the aged grandmother with whom she shared her life had charged her with a growing burden of labour: it was hardly surprising that she felt indisposed to further exertion. Hence, the daily walks in the forest to which she was accustomed had grown ever shorter.

She lay with no coverlet – regardless of the daylight and open air – subject to the gaze of any passer-by and convenient for the lustful intentions of any rogue. Yet when she had laid herself in this supine position earlier to rest her tired limbs, she had felt no apprehension, she had not been conscious of the vulnerability of her exposed position. For she was uninformed as to the meaning of lust, unaware that young ladies might need to protect themselves from it. Given the isolation of her existence, it was understandable that she should be in this manner innocent of the ways of the world. To brand her as lacking in modesty or as brazen would involve a misunderstanding of her nature: this maiden was extremely modest. Furthermore, it simply had not occurred to her that anyone might pass by: after all, she frequented the loneliest areas of the forest in her wanderings and in years had scarcely chanced upon a soul, an occasional solitary woodcutter perhaps, who, absorbed in his task, had barely remarked her fleeting presence.

Her grandmother had issued her with many warnings, of course, but the warnings, unlike the traditional admonitions of old women towards their granddaughters, had not concerned the perfidious or salacious nature of men – partly, no doubt, because this granddaughter, unlike others, as yet had demonstrated no interest in the subject; partly, also, because Grandmother herself had apparently suffered no souring experience. The warnings concerned instead the nature of the forest.

Grandmother maintained that there was a dark mysterious undercurrent to the forest, beyond the comprehension of any human, and that it was not to be trusted. Whilst allowing her ward to roam freely, the old woman urged her always to be home by sunset and to return immediately should there be any change in the weather. She would explain that the forest was ageless, that it had existed long before the human race and that it knew more than people ever could: it held secrets about past, present and future, about the creation of humanity and about its destiny. Yet all this special knowledge, she contended, the forest reserved for itself, barring even humans from it and exploiting it for its own devices.

The young girl listened attentively, by nature a courteous child, and always followed her grandmother's instructions, though secretly discounting the concern for her safety. For she possessed a deep faith in the eternal benevolence of the forest: the mysteries which her grandmother hinted at merely added intensity to her feeling. And so, as she slumbered upon her bed of moss, no fear of forest, or of man or woman, troubled her; she lay lost in contented dreams.

Her name was Floretta and she was indeed as delightful as a little flower: her skin was as soft as the most delicate of petals and her lips were as rich as the warmest pink rose; her lively sparkling eyes, for the moment veiled in slumber, possessed the tender blue-green of sylvan banks thick with spring bluebells; her serene contented face was like the crowning glory of a fresh bloom on any lovely flower. This resemblance to a flower was not coincidental, for Floretta was indeed a child of the forest in which she lived.

She was fully aware of her origin: hence her great love for the forest. Grandmother shared this awareness, and from this knowledge stemmed her apprehension: she feared that Floretta would share the fate of her own daughter Flora – Floretta's mother – who had been the forest's lover. It was her belief that the forest could become too possessive with the ones it loved, and she would recount how the forest had taken her dearest Flora from her, one winter's day, when Floretta was still only a small babe – it was as if the forest had been jealous of the attention that Flora needed to pay her child. Grandmother's final point – which she never failed to emphasise – was how little concern the forest had shown for the welfare of its offspring at that stage.

Floretta, however, saw abundant evidence of her father's concern: her father the forest had, after all, in its turn issued her with warnings: it had cautioned her as to the many foibles of humankind in preparation for trials awaiting her in the World of Man.

As she stirred now from her welcome rest, her waking thoughts were as blissful as had been her dreams: no fleeting disquietude marred her sublime tranquillity. The contradictory influences to which she had been subjected had not made her an anxious child and she was as untroubled now by the forest's warnings concerning humankind as she had always been by her grandmother's vituperative arraignment of the forest: the prospect of straying forth from the forest's secure dominion appeared remote: she had experienced no desire – and as yet conceived of no need – to do so.

Thinking to wend homeward, she rose, and in rising, her soft thick hair forsook its sunflower arrangement and fell instead loosely about her shoulders so that her facial lineaments became obscured. But that part only of her beauty became hidden: her change of position had revealed much more: uprightness became her better: stronger appeared her affinity with the forest, more evident those physical features which were derived from the forest trees: her body now stood as slim and lithe as the most graceful silver birch; her movement now showed itself as smooth and undulant, like the gentle motion of branches swaying under the caress of a summer breeze; her hair, forever apparent, gleaming in sunlight or in the darkest shade, was the colour of autumnal gold.

CHAPTER 2

Forth from her quiet darkened cottage, Floretta set out boldly on an unexpected journey: through the dawning forest and beyond – into the World of Man. She had prepared herself with no special grooming and had selected no luggage.

The day promised to be fine and friendly: the early morning sun shone mottled through the trees, the breeze, still cool, was gentle and refreshing, and on such days Floretta's lithe body would move easily and gaily like a dancing flicker of golden light in and out between the thick trunks of the trees. But on this day, her movement was stumbling and laboured as if she were experiencing great difficulty or pain.

She took no rest. Forced onwards by the urgency and panic of human emotion, she struggled on along the rough path, pushing aside the thorny branches which contrived to block her way. Such frustration, such confusion she had never known before: a strange conflict of loyalties was tearing at her heart; for the first time ever, she had defied the forest, ignored its blandishments, disobeyed its entreaty to stop, stop, and follow a different path.

"Oh, forest!" she called. "I am your child, a child of the forest, this I know, but I am also a human being! I cannot always follow you! Sometimes I must forget you, and forget myself! I have given you my complete devotion in the past and will do so again in times to come, but for this moment at least, I must turn away from you towards humankind…"

But now she had to halt. A thicket of holly bushes which she had never noticed growing in this area of the forest before was now completely obstructing any further progress.

"Trees, oh trees!" she cried out in anguish. "Tear down your thorny bushes and allow me through! You know the urgency of my errand! I have no time to lose…"

A stronger wind blew, a rush of cooling air, ruffling Floretta's golden tresses, and then came the low unhurried voice of the forest: "Little one, dear child, calm yourself… Become still, as still as the trees… Abandon your futile task and follow where we lead. This track is now quite impassable, it is completely overgrown…"

"Only through your doing!" she cried.

"No child, not through our doing, but essentially through the passage of time. It is many years now since this path was last trod. If you persevere, you will arrive too late. You cannot go where you intend. We must show you another path."

"How can there be another path?"

"Dear child! What must we do to make you listen? How can we lead you where you must but will not go? We would prefer to guide you rather than to force you, but we cannot lead if you will not follow…"

But Floretta was not listening; she was distracted by an intense feeling of disillusionment. "I was warned and now I understand," she cried. "Oh, forest, you are becoming too possessive of me! I discounted all the warnings, I did not believe this time would ever come, but I see it now! You are jealous of my connections with the World of Man. You have no care for any human being, however dear to me, and resent their warning against you. You will not help me! I must help myself!"

She left the path and wandered to the left, hoping to find some route around the holly bushes and to rejoin the trail beyond. But even as she did this, more of the prickly shrubs appeared before her. She gasped and turned and ran instead to the right of the thicket. In this direction, the holly hedge seemed to continue into the forest as far as the eye could see, forming an awesome and impenetrable barrier.

Hesitating for one moment only, she stepped forward and tore desperately at the stiff branches of the holly bushes, scratching her gentle hands so that the blood of her fingers ran freely and mingled with the bright red berries. She did not cry out in pain. When she spoke again, her voice was quiet and sad. "Move your bushes aside," she implored. "Move them aside or I will fight my way through. I do not care if I cause myself injury."

"Child," replied the forest. "You are blinded by human panic and distracted from reason. Sadly, we must use force to protect you from suffering from your error. Thankfully, you will understand in time why we do this, and forgive us."

Upon these words, the bush in which Floretta had become entangled with a startling suddenness vanished, but as this happened, the ground began to rumble and to shake. Great tree trunks were heaving and lifting the soil around themselves, tearing their strong roots free from the depths of the earth so that cracks gaped and the ground crumbled down into them. And then the trunks came crashing down, ripping whole branches from neighbouring trees as they fell. The forest floor reverberated anew with the terrible force of each impact.

Progress forward was now obstructed by a massive trunk, too thick to surmount and of tremendous length, which had fallen so alarmingly close that the poor girl had covered her head with her arms and was now just biding her time and praying that the tumult would quickly abate. No need to look to the left. A resounding crash told her that direction too would be blocked. Another crash, and another. Movement to the right was likewise impossible.

She pressed her palms tightly upon her ears to protect them from this deafening assault, and a further shuddering of the earth told her there would be no escape behind. Until then, she had spared no thought for herself, but now her human emotions directed that she was afraid. What was to become of her? Was this the terrible fate against which she had always been warned?

She did not realise at once that the uproar had ceased. At last, opening her eyes once more very cautiously, she looked up and span round and then spied just one small gap in the surrounding stockade. As she headed for it, she felt the low branches of the fallen trees begin to touch and to prod her, but now no longer forcefully, instead so very tenderly, tenderly she realised, and so very lovingly.

Now the forest spoke again, and this time his voice was even more quiet and soothing than before. "Don't be afraid, little one. In your heart is only goodness and innocence. But you must learn to grow very strong, for in your life you will be confronted with great evil…"

Subdued now, and weary and tattered, Floretta obediently followed the route along which the branches prompted her. The way was quite clear before her; the branches moved upwards or to the side so as to make a path and avoid brushing against her scratched and sore body.

"Dear child," whispered the trees, as much to each other as to their beloved daughter, "you will learn in time, and we hope today, that there is no conflict between the interests of humankind and the interests of the forest. The conflict is an illusion. To honour the forest is to serve the needs of humankind. Can you see that, little one? It is simply that people with their short lives are fascinated by trivialities and preoccupied with individuals. They cannot view humanity as a whole, they cannot identify their needs with the needs of their community, whereas the forest… The forest can see itself as an entity. The trees see themselves at once as many and as one. And the forest can view a so much longer span of time… Remember…

"Remember, the forest witnessed the birth of humankind. And if ever humankind is no more, be sure that the forest will still be here. The human race may destroy itself, it may destroy the forest, but then with time there would come more forest. We do not wish the human race to destroy itself, we wish it well, but wishing has no substance. We have always watched people deceiving themselves and have grieved for them. But our grief has no power. We know by what means they could attain their highest goals and we could advise them. But they would not listen and then would not understand… Do you understand, dearest child, at least a little of what we say?"

Floretta only partly understood these ideas; her tired mind could not concentrate fully on the forest's words; she merely half-listened, soothed by his gentleness. What she did understand was the love in his quiet tone and she trusted him now. The pain of her confusion was gone.

"Humanity…" continued the forest, seeking perhaps more to soothe than to clarify. "Humanity troubles itself with matters which successive generations will soon have forgotten, and of which only the trees will retain any memory. Human beings neglect the central tasks of their group and busy themselves with activities which leave a bad legacy for others, whilst imagining that they do themselves good. And this too is only because humanity is trapped within the separateness of each individual, restricted by the shortness of each individual's time…

"But remember, little one, you need not feel the pressures of time. You are of the forest, the ageless, timeless forest. You are a link between two worlds – you are human but, alone among humans, you remain free from preoccupation with your own identity. In this, you are a truly wonderful child, truly wonderful, but quite unmoved by yourself…"

* * * * *

The path along which Floretta was guided was long and penetrated ever deeper into the densest parts of the forest. She had rarely ventured so far before. The branches encouraged her onwards, ever higher, always climbing, leading her between bushes, over brooks and rocky crags, far from any beaten trail. She began to feel expectant, as if something special were about to happen.

Then the branches ceased their prompting.

"Behind these rocks," whispered the trees, "and beneath the exposed roots of the old oak that straddles them is a little hollow, hidden away, with room just for one. You are expected. We only wish we could have brought you here more easily – you would have come at once if you had known. But the secret of this place could not be anticipated."

Eager and curious, she clambered over the rocks and down into the mossy dip. At once she was spellbound. She gasped. For, growing there on a little hump was the most wonderful flower she had ever seen. It was a simple flower, just a single bloom possessing only five large oval petals, but it was incredibly beautiful.

At first glance, it was seen to glow a deep rich red, but then the little one found herself deceived, for the flower revealed itself the purple of a gleaming amethyst, and then at once it had changed again and was now a bright blue as of the finest sapphires and now the soft azure of summer skies. The little one knelt down and gazed in adoration at it. Only its centre, she noticed, was unchanging; it seemed to radiate the power of goodness: its heart was the colour of purest gold.

CHAPTER 3

In accordance with the flower's instructions, Floretta had carefully uprooted it and taken it home and positioned it – housed in a suitable pot – upon her grandmother's window sill.

Shortly before they had reached the cottage, the flower had thought to bind Floretta to secrecy: "No one must know that I can speak," it had declared. "You must tell no one, not even your grandmother. Speak to me if you wish, but only as you might any flower, with no substance in your words. I wish no special treatment – water me sparingly, this is all I ask."

Floretta had found Grandmother lying upon her bedroom floor beside a disarrayed bed, motionless and cold, an equally cold counterpane wrapped vainly about her. She had experienced no surprise or shock, however, for she quite expected to find matters so – it was in search of a surgeon or apothecary to attend her grandmother that she had originally been driven forth. Neither was she dismayed by the lack of change, as she might well have been, for hope now burned in her heart: instantly upon discovering the iridescent flower, her worst fears had been dispelled: she had experienced a spiritual uplifting, for the flower inspired confidence, it granted peace, it extended a beneficent, an ameliorative influence.

And then she had regretted her foolish behaviour, realising with the shrewd insight of retrospect that the forest had merely been attempting to lead her to the flower and that she with her feeble objections had merely caused unnecessary delay; realising too that, even if the forest had explained its intention, she would still have been suspicious and uncooperative. For the magic of this flower could indeed only be truly appreciated by those who had seen it; before seeing it, she herself would not have believed.

She understood now more of what her father the forest had attempted to tell her and could conceive that the goodness of the forest extended far beyond human comprehension; she determined never again to permit any inroad on her faith.

After positioning the flower in the morning sun and regarding her grandmother ruefully, Floretta had gone to tidy herself: only now had she come to realise the extreme unkemptness of her appearance.

Needless to say, she did not wish her grandmother to see her in this state. As she washed her tired and sullied limbs, she noticed something rather surprising: the scratches and bruises she was sure she had collected earlier appeared to have healed. This made her quarrel with the forest seem unreal, fictional – a pleasing notion.

As she searched for any remaining sign of injury, she heard a flustered voice from within: "Floretta, Floretta? Where are you, child? I seem to have slipped out of bed – come and help me back in, will you? My goodness! What time of day is it?"

* * * * *

Within days Grandmother felt her leg strong enough to stand on and so, ignoring Floretta's protests, forsook her bed. To begin with, she just sat outside in the sun enjoying the long summer days, but soon she took to helping Floretta with some of the chores. Floretta insisted there was no need for this unless Grandmother really wanted to, and Grandmother in turn insisted that she really did want to. She enjoyed working. Or so she said. And she did indeed look so strong and healthy that Floretta could find no reason to prevent her. Her back seemed straighter nowadays and her hands weren't nearly so stiff. She had regained quite a lot of the vigour which many years before had so characterised her. Her activity evoked in Floretta memories of her earlier childhood, memories of the woman her grandmother had once been.

If Floretta remarked, "Goodness, you are looking well, Grandmother," Grandmother would reply, "Yes, it's this good summer we're having. The sunshine loosens my joints…" or sometimes, "Yes, it's all the exercise I've been getting lately. I must say, I was rather inactive last winter. Won't let myself get like it again…"

Never did she indicate the least suspicion that there might be some magical reason for her splendid health. She had noticed the iridescent flower, of course, and had remarked on it, but had omitted to consider it anything extraordinary.

"That's a pretty flower," she had said casually. "Haven't seen one like that before. Did you find it in the forest?"

Several months had passed and winter had begun to set in before Floretta had come to realise that without any doubt Grandmother was indeed growing younger, not merely becoming a healthier old woman, but changing back into the sort of woman she had to have been in her earlier life. She now looked scarcely more than fifty. And, most striking, not only was she becoming physically younger and more energetic, her whole outlook was becoming that of a younger person: in her old age, Grandmother had become a rather droll old woman, obstinate though in a sweet-natured way, whereas she was now assuming a much more sensible and businesslike attitude. The stubbornness of old age appeared gone.

Floretta wondered what, if anything, she should say or do about this startling rejuvenation. There were no such drastic changes in Floretta herself for Grandmother to remark on – she had not become a little girl again but continued to develop daily as a young lady – but it seemed to Floretta that Grandmother must soon offer witness to the miracle that was manifest in herself. Having no mirror, Grandmother was unable to observe the transformation of her face: the gradual but tangible smoothing out of her wrinkles, the concomitant new youth of her complexion, which had discarded its parched senile yellow in favour of a more becoming fresh and creamy tone. These changes, Floretta realised, might well have escaped her notice, but the changes in her hands she could scarcely have ignored: her hands occupied her attention day long; they were the focus of her being; no longer stiff and arthritic, they were capable and productive once more.

And she was also able to study her hair: Floretta had for many years plaited her long white hair for her, but she had now reverted to arranging it herself – sometimes in more adventurous styles – so that she must have noticed that it was fast resuming its youthful red-gold.

But curiously, no acknowledgement of any of these changes passed Grandmother's lips. Floretta speculated that she did perhaps suspect magic but withdrew from expressing her suspicion for fear of weakening the spell – such was the belief of those times and Floretta herself was loath to put its truth to test.

That winter, their two pairs of able hands soon completed the chores and found themselves empty and restless during the long dark evenings: Grandmother became seized with a rush of creative activity in which she commenced a resurrection of the many useful crafts she had practised in her youth. In weeks she had consumed the stock of flaxen thread which Floretta had been busy spinning all summer. From it she wove a vast quantity of linen cloth – of varying thicknesses and qualities – some rough, some fine, all very strong. Using as a base some of the coarser of her newly woven cloth and employing offcuts from various exhausted articles of clothing, she created rag rugs, which often bore pleasing designs despite the limitations of her resources and with which she proudly adorned floor and walls, thereby contributing cosiness and style to the cottage and insulating them further from the veritable glacier without.

Next, the stack of logs beside the hearth became the object of her industrious zeal: selecting soft pieces of fine-grained wood, she carved new spoons, ladles, spatulas, to accoutre their kitchen, and then, frivolously, sculpted wooden clogs (for ornament only) and fashioned combs and clasps for the hair.

"When spring comes," she told Floretta, "we must find some clay and mould some new pots. And we must gather some rushes for mats for the scullery. Our household is growing very shabby. We have been very lax…"

And so, when spring came, Floretta learned where to find the best clay, how to knead it and shape the pots and how to bake them; she learned which reeds to choose to make the strongest and smartest mats. She learned too how to cut the cloth which Grandmother had woven and how to sew the pieces into clothes – plus which fabric suited which purpose – lessons all of which were long overdue, delayed until then solely by reason of Grandmother's previous inactivity.

Their beds too were needful of renovation. They saved the feathers from their hen house until there were sufficient to fill new pillows and they replenished their mattresses with fresh dry straw.

"When we have spun some more thread, I will teach you how to make lace," said Grandmother one day. "And when we have woven more cloth I will show you how to make the dyes to brighten it and the perfumes to enhance it: the essence of pine cone I suggest for men, and for women the scents of the sweetest forest flowers."

One morning in April as she sorted through their needlework, Floretta remarked, "Goodness, Grandmother, we have been busy. I cannot imagine how we will ever use all these things ourselves."

"When we have accumulated something of a stock," answered Grandmother, "we can take our wares to the market at Torquella. Such a grand occasion!"

Floretta was taken by surprise: "But Grandmother, I thought you didn't like going all the way to Torquella."

"Nonsense. Whatever gave you that idea? I will admit it's quite a distance, but then Torquella is a fine town and well worth visiting. We could manage it: before we go we will have to make ourselves bark baskets to carry our goods. Ah, how thrilling it will be… You will love it, child – all the excitement and merriment… And we'll be able to buy all sorts of lovely things that we usually have to do without."

After this, preparations for market day occupied Grandmother's whole interest. She decorated some of the fine linen shirts they had made with lace so they would command a better price and embroidered others with fine-spun threads dyed the bright colours of the forest berries, working the most exquisite of rustic patterns with her nimble fingers. She spoke frequently of the market now and sought to rouse Floretta's enthusiasm – for, though making a polite attempt, Floretta did not entirely share in the joyful anticipation.

"Ah, child, I've kept you too long in this backwood," Grandmother assured her. "You cannot imagine what you have missed. I only hope the thrill of the town won't go to your head."

Floretta felt sure it would not. She was a child of the forest and here her heart would always remain, with the countryside, with the trees. She wasn't at all sure she would like the town. Her misgivings she concealed from Grandmother as best she could. For it was Grandmother who, after all, was the object of her concern. Grandmother had once known many people from Torquella. Would any of them still be alive? Would they now recognise her? If they did, would they suspect what had happened? If so, what would they think? Would they suspect witchcraft? How would they react to this? What would they do? What would they say?

Floretta was perplexed, and so resolved to obtain an audience with the flower, though to respect its injunction to silence in doing so. Consequently, she contrived to be alone with the flower: when Grandmother had cause to venture out into the forest, Floretta, unusually, found reason to stay in. Approaching the flower in its now permanent position on her grandmother's window sill, eager and yet reluctant to address it, she experienced a sense of blessed relief when she heard it address her first.

"Ah, there you are," said the flower. "I agree, it is time we spoke. Many weeks have now passed. Hear this, Floretta, you need have no fear for your grandmother. She will come to no harm. Her life will run its natural course and meet no untimely interruption. Is that what you wanted to know?"

"Yes, dearest flower," answered Floretta. "That is exactly what I wanted to know. You place my mind at rest."

From then on, Floretta began looking forward to the forthcoming visit, now that she knew there to be no danger awaiting Grandmother in

Torquella. It did not occur to this selfless and gentle girl that neither she nor the flower had considered the question of whether she herself would be placed in danger.

CHAPTER 4

To reach their destination it was required of them to surmount a steep ridge, for the town of Torquella was situated some five miles away in the next valley. The alternative might have been to follow the brook which flowed near their cottage to its eventual confluence with the great river – the River Tor – and thereafter to continue along the riverbank for some miles. This would lead at length to the heart of the town – and would have been downstream and downhill all the way – but would have entailed a considerable detour along tracks which were even less frequently trod than the one they chose.

The way uphill proved arduous, for the path was indeed so overgrown that, had they been less accustomed to the forest, they might well either have lost their way or else have abandoned their scheme and returned home: each was further encumbered by two heavy baskets suspended from a yoke. Neither felt daunted however: the two were in full agreement that it was high time for this trail to be forged again, and the forest apparently shared this sentiment, for it placed no obstacles in their path and moved branches aside for them wherever it might assist their passage.

When they reached the top of the ridge, the worst was behind them, for their steep, rough, winding track soon joined a wider and smoother path which set about gradually looping its way down the hillside. They were still deep in the forest, however, so that their range of vision was restricted by shrubs and the tops of trees, but in time, as they gained ground, the forest thinned and they were granted far views across the valley to other distant wooded slopes.

It was not long before Floretta caught her first glimpse of the milk-white towers and biscuit-coloured roofs of Torquella, nestling deep down in the valley. Strangely, this captivating mirage drew no closer as they progressed along their path, but then, to have headed directly for it would have entailed leaving the path and risking their lives in a foolhardy descent of the steep slope at their side. The ridge here ran parallel to the great river which gave the kingdom of Torquella its strength – and its name – and which nurtured its fair city (of the same name), and so they could only continue along the trail countless others before them had blazed, however indirect its path might seem.

Despite its breadth, the river was not here visible in its entirety, only stretches appearing occasionally between the rooftops and the abundant foliage. As Floretta looked down on the city with its gables, turrets, treetops and glimpses of silver water, she felt a surge of strange emotion – an expectancy, which quickened her pace, and then an uncertainty, which checked it. So this was the World of Man!

And yet all was so still in the valley that, from this distance, it appeared conceivable that the town was no longer inhabited; that, at some time, the peace and dignity of the forest had pervaded the town, precluding the clamour by which humans lived and thrived. If this were so, where might the disinherited humans have gone? Forth with resignation into the forest, prepared now to live by the forest's conditions or intending merely to wrench another town from the fabric of the forest?

As she plodded resolutely, Floretta began almost to consider seriously that the town might be deserted and that their tiring journey would prove all in vain. But ere these strange thoughts had had time to establish themselves, a sonorous pealing of bells broke out and began echoing and re-echoing across the valley as if to confirm humankind's supremacy, to confirm that the domain of the forest still ended with the last great tree and first house.

"How wonderful to hear the sound of bells!" exclaimed Grandmother, interrupting Floretta's train of thought. "You know, Floretta, for all the bells to be rung at once like this, something really special must have happened!"

As they descended, they lost sight of the town, though never leaving earshot of the bells. Their path grew even steeper and it became necessary to negotiate a few hazardous bends. But then they found they had reached the bottom: their path converged on another wider one, which in turn grew wider still as yet more paths contributed to it. Their own original track was now left far behind; they were traversing the territory of folk unknown; they were nearing habitation. And so they found that they themselves were only two amongst many travellers making use of these byways.

Despite their own unhurried step, they caught up and overtook a peasant and his lad driving three sheep and a cow. These poor scraggy beasts could obviously sense that some change of fate was awaiting them (and more likely for the worse), for they ambled at an insolently slow pace despite their master's exhortations to hurry.

"Good day," muttered the man casually as the two passed and then, looking up and noticing Floretta, cast eyes suddenly lascivious upon her and added earnestly, "My, you've a fine lass there, Ma'am. Good day to you too, Miss!" And both father and son grinned, their faces becoming consumed with the uncontrolled and ill-concealed lust of simpletons.

"Good day," replied Floretta shyly, attempting to reciprocate what she had perceived as friendliness, quite innocent of the significance of their reactions. Not only had her secluded life protected her from knowledge or experience of lechery, she had been spared vanity through never having observed her face in a mirror, though she had at times glimpsed an imperfect reflection of herself when the quiet waters of small summer streams had stilled to glasslike smoothness.

The two herds were soon left behind.

Next it was Grandmother and Floretta's turn to be overtaken, and by a pedlar riding in a donkey cart, his wares jangling as he journeyed and thereby heralding his approach, so that the two turned to watch him pass. "Good day," he called gaily as he sped by. But his face seemed to light up as he spotted Floretta. "Whoa!" he called at once to his surprised donkey, tugging abruptly on the reins.

"Good day, Ma'am," he said when the two drew level with him again, addressing Grandmother even though his eyes were on Floretta. "I must say, Ma'am, you have a very lovely daughter."

"Goodness no," laughed Grandmother. "This is my granddaughter!"

"Indeed!?" he marvelled. "Then the child must be a deal younger than she looks. No matter. But perhaps she would like a ribbon for her lovely hair. Here, take this, little one. This colour will become you." He handed Floretta a blue ribbon and shook the reins to stir his donkey, but seemed reluctant to depart. "I must be off…" he said. "But let us hope we'll meet again…"

Now he addressed Floretta directly: "I'd take thee with me if I thought I could keep thee with me for long. But… as soon as I became fond of thee I would lose thee and be left with just a thorn and no longer a rose in my heart…" Then he shook his reins once more and jangled speedily on his way.

"A strange man," said Floretta. "Tell me, Grandmother, are all men so strange?"

"Aye, that they are," answered Grandmother, somehow absently. "Anyway, at least we now know for certain that today is market day. I would not wish our long journey to be for naught."

The path grew ever more thickly peopled; men, women, boys and girls, all heading for the market at an enthusiastic pace. They came upon a group of clownish dwarfs who seemed intent on practising their tumbling and buffoonery as they went, hoping no doubt to be on good form and earn fair sums for their efforts in the market place. They passed a trio of gaily clad jesters at the roadside, absorbed in servicing and tuning their collection of instruments. And they chanced upon groups of honest country folk like themselves, bearing the produce of many hours of patient skilled labour. Carts of fruit and vegetables passed them by, all destined of course for the fine market place of Torquella.

CHAPTER 5

As they entered the metropolis, the bells were still ringing, loudly and gaily, and it became increasingly clear that not just one but all the bell towers of the vicinage were joined in this harmonious cacophony. Their message was surely a joyful one and, as groups of people made their way along the streets in the direction of the market, Grandmother approached a friendly-looking peasant woman to inquire what the joyful message might be.

"Hast thou not heard?" answered the woman. "The Crown Prince Julien is betrothed at long last. The King will be relieved, I must say – they have searched ten kingdoms to find a princess to suit the whims of that lad! The news was announced from the Palace this morning at dawn, so they tell me."

"Well, that's glad news indeed," remarked Grandmother. "No wonder the bells ring so loud. Do you hear, Floretta? The Crown Prince is to marry and the Royal Line will continue. Today is a glad day for Torquella."

"A glad day for some…" The old wife sounded dubious. "Though maybe not for Torquella. A glad day for the King right enough – they say he feared his son would never marry. He's a flighty lad that one, but don't repeat me on that, wilt thou? They say the King feared he would never see a royal grandson." She placed her hand across her mouth and lowered her voice. "Though bastard heirs enough his son has produced already to be sure. But don't say as 'twas me that told thee."

"That I won't," said Grandmother.

"It's a glad day too for Her Royal Highness the Princess Lilibelle: now that her brother is marrying, she will be allowed to find a suitor herself. A wait of many more years and she would have found the task well nigh impossible, princess or no princess, wealthy or not, for she is ugly enough already."

"Indeed?" remarked Grandmother. "I have never seen Lilibelle."

"Hast thou not? Some say the King will arrange a match with her cousin, the Prince Elbert. If so, she'll do well – he's a handsome lad, but another flighty one, they say… I dare say he won't be pleased at the prospect though. If he has any sense he will find himself a fair match in haste before his father and the King get their heads together…"

32

"Tut, tut," said Grandmother. "What goings-on in the Royal Household! I had no idea things had come to such a pass."

"Aye, much has changed in Torquella these years, and fast," continued the old gossip. "What I could tell thee if I had all day! Thy ears wouldn't believe the half of it…"

"Indeed?"

"Aye, take my advice and be wary in this town. Trust no one except thy own kind…"

On this cautionary note, the woman broke off and rejoined the group of peasant women she was journeying with. Her lively voice could soon be heard once more as it contributed to the babble of their idle tattle.

They moved with the direction of the crowd and at length ascended the incline to the old stone bridge. The high bridge granted fine views over the riverside area of the town against the backdrop of the hills and mountains beyond, where the Tor was known to have its source. On the lesser side, the left bank, which they were just leaving, the tall houses were constructed up to the water's edge, some even overhanging it, while on the other bank the buildings – warehouses rather than dwellings – were set back behind a substantial waterfront. But they did not dally. They crossed quickly over the mighty river and proceeded a way along the quay past the assortment of small craft moored there. One more corner and they had reached the market place.

Floretta's first impression was of its great size. It was huge – far larger than her dim childhood memories would have had her believe. Her second impression was of how full it was with people. The great size of the square was clearly needed. The place was crawling with activity, as hundreds of merchants, pedlars and country folk hastily erected their trestles and arranged their wares. The regular traders had booths with brightly coloured awnings, but the nomads and casuals were organising their goods as best they might upon the cobbles. Everyone was working furiously, hoping no doubt to catch the trade of the earliest shoppers.

Having reached the bottom corner of the square, Floretta and Grandmother rested their baskets on the ground while they caught their breath. To their right, the market square was open to the river – the quay continued along here – while to their left it was bounded by a long terrace of rather fine colonnaded houses. Floretta knew there to be another terrace of equal worth facing it, but the square was so packed it was only partially visible. Pride of place at the top of the square, she could remember, was held by the elegant buildings of the Royal Palace – for the moment all but obscured.

"We'd best stroll around first," said Grandmother. "It's so long since I was here I have no idea how to price our goods. I think we need to consider the prices for work like our own and then we can decide how much we dare charge."

But as they walked along past the quickly growing stalls, it was instead work unlike their own which caught Floretta's eye. Such was the variety of exotic and colourful goods that she found it hard to concentrate on a routine search for country needlecraft like their own. Fruit and vegetables and potted plants were abundant, but most exciting were those goods which she could not remember ever having set eyes on before.

She was attracted by the tinker's stall bedecked with shining copper pans and gleaming silver spoons, all the more brilliant in the sunlight alongside dull-faced pewter mugs. And then by a woodworker's stall adorned with handmade musical instruments of all sizes and various families, each instrument differing slightly from its immediate neighbour: at the front the wind family with pipes long and short, some curved, some straight, some with as many as twenty finger-holes but others with just one; and behind these, the string family with viols round and fat, square and flat, or even hexagonal. The woodworker had arranged his stall and was already attracting custom by playing a merry little tune on each of his strange instruments in turn.

"Oh, Grandmother," asked Floretta. "Can't we stop and watch a while?"

"No, child, that we can't." This was the voice of experience. "Not if we want to be able to purchase later. Remember, we have no coin. And if we dally any longer, there will soon be none to be had…" Able to pass the stalls by without being unduly distracted, Grandmother had soon gleaned the information she required: "Our work is good," she told Floretta. "Much of what I have seen does not rival it. If we choose a good spot, we should get a fair price."

Grandmother found them an unused pitch at the top of a row, verging on the Palace square, just a stone's throw from the Palace gates. The adjacent stall was that of a herbalist. Floretta eyed his wares with interest – snippets of fresh herbs in bunches arranged at the front; behind these, spices and the rough powders of dried leaves in jars; and at the back, large slim-necked decanters containing strange potions from which the herbalist was filling smaller bottles. As he poured, vapours arose and filled the air with aromas intoxicatingly sweet or chokingly pungent.

Grandmother did not reprove Floretta for her curiosity and for the small part she was playing in their work, but seemed to expect it, and proceeded herself with the business of selling. She had already sold one of their fine shirts and several simple aprons, and another prospective customer was approaching her.

"Tell me," said this person sideways, giving utterance somehow without moving his lips as if to convince any onlooker that he was not in fact speaking. "Tell me. I part not with my hard-earned coin." He jingled the large purse hanging from his belt. "I offer instead protection, in exchange for your wares."

"Protection?" responded Grandmother. "I need none."

"Don't you believe it, Ma'am," said he. "That you do. As yet you have few coins, but when you have disposed of your wares and earned many, you will not keep them long without my protection."

"Rubbish!" retorted Grandmother. "Be off with you! If I need protection, it's not from thieves but from lying tricksters like you!"

Floretta was no longer mesmerised by the herbalist; her attention had been seized by the altercation developing in front of her.

"Madam, you misjudge me!" the 'lying trickster' declared. "For the price of just one fine shirt, I will mingle with the crowd, sneak in the shadows and ever be ready to spring to your aid, whilst you scarce know I am there… Have you not seen the way the caravan merchants eye your magnificent daughter? And, if I may say it, you are a fine figure of a woman yourself…"

"You may not say it!"

"Ah, but Madam, I must say it, as you seem so ill-informed. I am referring of course to slavery…"

"Slavery?" An edge to Grandmother's voice betrayed the shock the word had given her, but she maintained her composure. "I know of none in Torquella. Be off with you, unless you desire to purchase." Her molester moved not the slightest, which only served to heighten her annoyance. "Be off with you! You are making me lose my customers!"

"As you wish," he replied. "I will leave you unguarded. I can see that you are stubborn. But accept some advice – and this I tender free of charge: do not stay abroad in Torquella after nightfall! The caravan merchants will be at large, hoping for easy prey…"

"But the King's Guard has always protected the people!" protested Grandmother.

"No longer! No longer!" he sneered. "Madam, just how little do you know? Do you not believe the stories you hear? Some dismiss it as rumour, but I know it for fact, that the Royal Household has taken slaves brought here from foreign parts… and in return allows the merchants the freedom to abduct as they wish."

Grandmother and Floretta looked at each other aghast, but before they had had a chance to question the vagabond, he had gone on his way and disappeared into the crowd.

"Grandmother, what did he mean?" asked Floretta. "Did he really mean that they… they steal and… and sell people here in Torquella?"

"So he said. But take no notice of him. He was merely attempting to trick us into giving him a shirt…"

The two attempted to forget the incident and applied themselves to selling. Their superb needlecraft was attracting attention and they were doing an extremely good trade. As their goods changed hands for gold and silver pieces, Grandmother slipped the coins into a purse hidden in the voluminous folds of her skirts.

As yet, they had seen no one they even remotely recognised, and Floretta was full of hope that the day would pass as such. So far at least, her worst fears had proved unfounded. Quite possibly, everyone had changed so much during the previous decade that even people they had known would no longer be recognisable and, equally, would not know them.

Examining the fine embroidered shirts now was a portly and elaborately attired gentleman attended by two huge eunuch bodyguards. He was clearly not a native of Torquella and could only be one of the aforementioned caravan merchants.

"Are you buying?" asked Grandmother. "The prices are very fair."

"Shirts? I think not," he answered. "Though I admire the handwork. But tell me, Madam, is your fine girl for sale? I will give you a very fair price for her…"

Grandmother was furious. "That she is not, Sir! Be off with you!"

The merchant laughed, quite unabashed. "Good lady!" he chuckled. "Do not underestimate me. I am quite serious! And I, Hannibal the Honest, am I so called for nothing? I consider myself fair. I give you the chance now of sale. My competitors would not give you that chance, but would merely await the opportunity of seizure… And they, dear lady, would not treat your girl as honourably as Hannibal the Honest!"

"Be off with you! Be off!"

"Certainly, if such is your desire. But, make no mistake, we will meet again…" With an irritating, sickly-sweet smile he departed and at a slow, shuffling pace, his movement restricted by his obesity, then followed at length by his two superbly formed attendants who bore aloft the large packages of his purchases.

Grandmother was clearly relieved when the group had finally disappeared. "Goodness, I cannot like these foreign merchants," she muttered, her voice wavering as she repressed her disgust. "Believe me, Floretta, we had less trade with them in Torquella ten years ago, and those that came were kept more in their place. Much more of this and we'll not come again." She applied herself to arranging and rearranging the remaining goods rather unnecessarily, as if trying to forget what had occurred.

"Maybe we should have accepted the offer of protection," suggested Floretta.

"Nonsense," Grandmother replied. "That rogue would not have protected us – even if we had given him every single shirt we possessed." She was clearly still annoyed.

"Stand aside! Stand aside!" This cry drew their attention from their wares again. "Stand aside for his Royal Highness the Prince Elbert!" This authoritative voice proved to be that of a boy. The people at once stood deferentially well back and allowed through a procession of two haughty little page-boys, a handsome prince and behind him, a pair of sturdy sword-bearing personal guards. Though fairly used to seeing their royalty at close quarters, the crowd were intrigued and gazed at their prince with curious and fascinated eyes.

The Prince approached Grandmother.

"Do you require shirts, Your Highness?" she inquired with noticeable aplomb.

"No, Madam. I come to address your daughter, whom I have been admiring from yonder these sixty minutes!" When he said 'yonder', he flicked his hand vaguely in the direction of the Royal Palace.

"Indeed?" responded Grandmother.

A murmur of wonder and yet approval came from the crowd as suddenly, after so little warning, the Prince fell upon one knee before Floretta and boldly took her hand.

"Maiden." He addressed her solemnly. "Beauty such as yours have I never seen. If you will come with me, I will dress you in satins and velvets and obtain for you the most priceless of jewels, the rarest and most exquisite of gems to complement your loveliness."

Thoroughly abashed, Floretta could merely stammer, "Sir, I beg your pardon most humbly, but I care not for fine clothes or jewels…"

The Prince glared but remained on one knee before her, his eyes searching her face, as if waiting for a quick change of heart.

"I cannot go with you…" she told him.

The crowd too waited in astonishment, but then someone could be heard to comment, "The conceit of the girl, that she counts herself too good for Prince Elbert."

And then the reply: "Exactly. What possesses her? She can aim no higher, not now Julien is betrothed."

Floretta sensed that she had committed the gravest of errors. She could see from the Prince's eyes that not only had she embarrassed him deeply on a personal level, she had humiliated him before his people. It was unpardonable. But what could she have done? She tried to save the situation: "Forgive me, My Lord," she pleaded. "I had no intention to displease you, but you took me so much by surprise…"

With cold eyes he stood and bowed formally, first to Floretta and then to Grandmother.

"Your Highness," said Grandmother. "Forgive my daughter. She is but a child, much too young to marry. Do not judge her age from her looks. She is a child and knows nothing of men."

"Quite so," he snapped. "She has the manners of an untrained infant." He turned on his heel and stalked off, followed by his retinue.

The crowd did not disperse at once but stood around discussing the affair, telling newcomers to the scene about it, staring at Floretta and pointing accusing fingers at her.

"I have had enough of this," said Grandmother. "My mind is made up. We have sold sufficient for one day. Let us pack up what remains, proceed with our own purchases and start for home."

CHAPTER 6

Whilst they were packing their wares away, they were pleased to sell a few more items, so that Grandmother was a little more cheerful by the time they were ready to move off.

"Now," she said brightly, "I have already decided what I want to buy and I know where to find it. First, we will purchase a good-sized bag of finely ground miller's flour, such as you will not remember ever having seen, Floretta. Compared with our own coarsely milled wheatmeal, it is a true luxury."

"Can we not buy something from the herbalist?" asked Floretta. "I have been watching his work all day."

"We have no need," answered Grandmother briskly. "Nothing ails us. We have no aches and pains. We do not need oil to lubricate our joints. And you have no need for his sickly potions. They are for the weak-spirited who must view the world through a false heavenly haze."

Grandmother hurried Floretta past the herbalist and on to the miller, where they purchased the fine flour with some of the gold and silver pieces they had earned. From him they also bought salt, a necessity of life and yet also a luxury, not yielded by the forest, likewise cane sugar with which they could sweeten their cooking and concoct delicious sweetmeats.

They passed a merchant selling fine fabrics of every lovely hue brought from foreign lands, pausing to feel the textures of the cloths but deciding it would be extravagant to buy. "We can weave our own cloth," reasoned Grandmother, "and tailor our own clothing. There is just one item of apparel we cannot so easily make for ourselves and that we will look for next. I wonder if you can guess, Floretta? Leather sandals like the old pair you are wearing today."

"Of course!" exclaimed Floretta.

"Strange," remarked Grandmother absently to herself. "Strange to think I bought that very pair for myself in this market place… it must be well over fifteen years ago now…"

They found the booth of a tanner and saddler and admired his collection of superb leather goods: sandals, shoes and boots; belts, purses, bags of all sizes and descriptions; saddles for horses and other beasts of burden; waistcoats, breeches and hats in shining leather or supple suede.

"We will take just two pairs of sandals," Grandmother told the old tanner.

"Two pair each," he stated craftily, wrinkling his wizened old face so that it too looked like tanned leather. "Two pair each. At three silver pieces a pair that makes twelve pieces."

"No!" Grandmother laughed. "Two pairs, not four: one pair each."

"Oh, I should take two pair each," he insisted. "Lovely sandals. Handmade. You won't find many like these in Torquella and I've nearly sold out. Not so active nowadays as I used to be."

"But we don't need two pairs each," Grandmother told him. "A pair lasts ten years – if not twenty. Why, look at the pair my daughter is wearing!" ("Daughter?" thought Floretta. It was at least the second time Grandmother had said it.) "I bought them for myself, why, it must be well over fifteen years ago, practically before she was born."

"That's right," agreed the tanner. "Flora? It was me that sold them to you those long years ago! I had an idea it was you, you know, but I couldn't be sure. You've changed so little in all this time, I must say, I thought it couldn't be you. And I did hear a rumour you'd died, I'm sure I did. Odd. I can't imagine how that rumour can ever have started, can you? Ella! Ella!" A little round woman, presumably his wife, emerged from behind the booth.

"Ella!" he told her. "Look who this is standing here before us now, so alive and so well, and so young! Flora Desylva!"

"Why so it is!" she assented. "Flora! After all this time! And this will be your own lovely daughter. How bonnie she is! You must be proud of her. How old will she be now?"

"I think I'm seventeen," contributed Floretta shyly.

"Seventeen years…" marvelled the tanner. "So long, Flora, since we've seen you…"

"I suppose your old mother will have passed on by now…" remarked the tanner's wife. Grandmother did not contradict this and Floretta dutifully made no comment.

"The old woodcutter Jerethim would have been glad to know his daughter Flora was still alive. It grieved him badly to hear otherwise, you know," continued the tanner. "He's passed on too now, of course. His wife as well, long ago. All the old ones are leaving us. But their son is alive and well. You should try and see him, Flora. He'd be glad to see you. His father must have spoken about you many times."

All this was news to Floretta: she had never heard of these people before.

"Well, I never!" said the wife. "I never thought to see Flora Desylva again. What a surprise! You must visit us…"

"Yes," agreed the tanner. "We still live in the same rooms, over my workshop. Here, take the sandals," he insisted, and would not accept payment.

Grandmother was clearly pleased to have met these old friends, but Floretta felt somehow disconcerted; she was concerned that questions she could not answer might be sprung upon her, and was glad to pass on to the other stalls. Next they visited the tinker's booth and bought some of the bright copper pans that had captured her attention earlier. As their sandals had been a gift, Grandmother felt they could after all afford some new pans. Their baskets were beginning to grow heavy again and their stock of gold and silver coins diminishing.

"Allow me to help you with your baskets," offered a rather frail old man, whom Floretta had noticed loitering and watching them while they selected their pots.

"There is no need," said Grandmother. "We can manage."

The old man searched her face closely. "I offer," he said, "because you remind me of a maiden I knew in my youth, many many years ago…"

"What was her name?"

"Alas, I've forgotten now…" he said sadly. "But, I admired her deeply. From afar, that is. I lost her, though I suppose she never was mine, to my cousin Jerethim the woodcutter, and she bore him a child. And then he lost her, for she wouldn't marry him. I never understood why…"

"That was me," said Grandmother quietly.

"How?" he asked. "How can it be? You're too young, far too young…"

Grandmother replied as if in a dream: "I've spent fifty years in the forest, bringing up my child and then my daughter's child, and in the forest all is peace and the time passes so slowly. And yet so quickly. A year could be as ten years or as ten minutes… I haven't aged in the forest. For me time has stood still."

"It's a miracle," he said. "Truly a miracle. It is you. And this little one, so lovely, so lovely, exactly as you were at her age… You know, I will tell everyone about you. It will thrill everyone to hear your story."

Floretta was astounded by this conversation and could only feel alarmed, certainly by the old man's promise to tell everyone. She longed to regain the familiar security of the forest. "Grandmother," she asked. "It is growing late. Do you think we had better be leaving?"

"A sensible child," said the old man. "You are right, my little one. It is dangerous to be abroad late in these times. I will accompany you both through the streets to the edge of town to help you with your baskets and there I will take my leave of you."

CHAPTER 7

Grandmother enjoyed talking to her old friend and even seemed sad to part from him, while Floretta was glad to reach the edge of town and to say goodbye. She felt a sense of relief on entering the forest once more, yet her mind was still far from at peace. There was so much she needed to ask Grandmother, yet knew that now was scarcely the time to initiate a discussion, not while they were both so tired. She herself was so exhausted she could hardly work out what exactly she needed to ask, though she had not forgotten that Grandmother had contradicted her own identity several times. This had however amounted to little more than agreeing with what other people had assumed; she was presumably simply protecting herself, though it was unlike her grandmother to dissemble.

They completed the flat straight stretch along the river valley with no problems and turned at last to ascend the ridge that stood between themselves and their home. Their journey now became truly arduous; though they had completed a similar stage on the other side of the ridge much earlier in the day, they had at that time been fresh, and that ascent had if anything been a lesser one. Floretta trudged on wearily, almost regretting now having parted from the old man, for he had at least helped with their baskets. She walked quietly, neither speaking to Grandmother nor Grandmother addressing her, not even really thinking, and almost drifting into a light sleep on her feet. Then she realised the trees were whispering an urgent message, and returned suddenly to full consciousness.

"Flora, Floretta… Listen, loved ones… Danger lies ahead, so you must be prepared. Do not be afraid, for we will protect you. But do not leave the main path. This hillside is so steep that you would place yourselves in greater danger…"

The forest did not elucidate, and they continued apprehensively on their way, treading more warily with each step and growing increasingly fearful of what might lie ahead. When eventually they rounded a bend, they found, apparently expecting them to pass this way – if not lying in wait for them – the two herdsmen they had passed in the valley that morning. They no longer had their beasts with them but instead pocketfuls of jingling coins, which apparently boosted their confidence and emboldened them.

"Stop, Floretta," said Grandmother quietly. "Don't go any closer to them. Move back slowly when they approach. Be careful. Keep your head. Don't excite them. Don't run."

The older herdsman approached, the lustful intentions written upon his face only partially disguised by the falling dusk. His son approached too… The two women stepped back. The herdsmen came closer… And again the women stepped back. Then the four stood quite still, poised either for attack or retreat, but waiting for the other side to move first. Into this silence came a distant thrumming sound and the four froze with the concentration of listening.

The sound grew louder and became recognisable as a clatter of horses approaching rapidly from the direction of town. The four rigid figures jerked to life; the two herdsmen panicked, conscious no doubt of the compromising position in which they had placed themselves, and ran this way and that, wondering whence they might escape, whether to climb the steep bank on one side or roll wildly down the slope on the other, while Floretta and Grandmother took this opportunity to rush past and gain some ground.

Floretta glanced back as the horses rounded the bend at speed. There were three of them. As their riders sighted her, they pulled to an abrupt halt: they knew her. She too knew them. Would they provide rescue, she asked herself, or did they represent additional danger? She suspected the latter: in their lead was the disagreeable caravan merchant who had attempted to 'purchase' her earlier.

"That's the girl!" the merchant cried. Apparently sensing the situation, he added, "Dispose of those two fools! They're of no value."

His two henchmen pulled long swords from long scabbards and edged their horses slowly forward, eyeing their quarry disdainfully from their superior position, calculating their attack. As the two herdsmen turned to flee, with two mighty sword sweeps their heads became severed and tumbled with their two bodies into the dust.

"Now the girl! But don't hurt her!" ordered the merchant. "I have been offered a fine price. And spare the woman. She should fetch something."

Floretta and Grandmother backed slowly away, sensing it would be quite futile to cast their baskets down and run: they themselves were quite powerless against these two murderous mounted giants and their ruthless master. Floretta could contain her terror no longer.

"Oh forest! Help us! Save us!" she cried.

Her words perplexed the riders and they halted their advance.

"Is this sorcery? Are they witches?" the eunuchs wondered together.

"You superstitious fools!" bawled their lord. "Are you frightened of a child? Seize her and let's be gone!"

Just then the earth groaned and shook, and the three horses whinnied and backed away. The riders fought to control them, but the beasts refused to co-operate as the earth heaved deeply. A great tree trunk came crashing down the steep hillside, casting before it cascades of rocks and boulders loosened from the tossing roots or displaced by the sweeping branches.

The two eunuchs retreated in the face of this onslaught, but the merchant obstinately tried to hold his ground. He dug his spurs into his stallion's flanks in an effort to force obedience, but the poor animal neighed in terror and reared up and threatened to throw off its weighty oppressor. The merchant found his whip and chastised his steed but failed to quieten it, seeming merely to terrorise it further.

The tree met the path at length with resounding force and finally came to rest across it, blocking the way and separating the merchant and his men from Floretta and Grandmother. Infuriated at seeing himself so easily deprived of such a valuable asset, the merchant fought harder to temper his animal and, at last succeeding, drew back a few yards before rushing at the obstructing trunk in an attempt to clear it.

The beast obediently jumped but, alas, the obstacle proved too high for it under the great weight of the obese merchant and as it jumped it failed to clear. It caught its rear hooves but still careered onward over the trunk, falling to one side, by chance to the downhill side of the path. As the horse rolled forward under its caving front legs, the merchant catapulted from his saddle and plunged headlong down the hillside, emitting a fearful cry as he fell to almost certain death below.

The liberated horse whinnied and squirmed but eventually found its footing and galloped off wild and terrified into the forest. The two eunuchs did not go to their master's aid. They demonstrated no such devotion. Instead, fearful perhaps of provoking further sorcery – spurred perhaps by their sudden taste of freedom – they turned on their horses and departed at top speed for town.

Grandmother and Floretta likewise left the scene post-haste and were glad to reach their cottage some time later without further incident. That night, for the first time in many years, Grandmother bolted the shutters tightly and barred the cottage door.

CHAPTER 8

There followed for Floretta a period of sadness such as she had not experienced in her life before. For she had observed the depths to which men could be driven by greed or lust; she had even seen men die at the hands of others in the service of these vices. Though instructive about the human condition, none of this was edifying and it was an ill force to be reckoned with. She distracted herself with a vigorous attack on such household tasks as presented themselves, and succeeded by such means in keeping discomposure at bay: externally, at least, she was quite serene.

Her priority was that she should do nothing to upset her dear grandmother, who did show signs of having been adversely affected by the happenings of that fateful day and who – it seemed to her – had already endured enough. For days now since their journey to market, Grandmother had kept the cottage well locked and had always found some reason to prevent Floretta from going out.

Yet though Grandmother expressed her response to events in actions, she did not express it in words; though the two women were incarcerated together, little discussion went on between them. Floretta might well have taken her grandmother to task, at least as to the meaning of the inconsistencies she had uttered concerning her identity, but shrank from so cruelly challenging her, willingly taking the greater part of the burden of their common distress on herself.

Being kept indoors quite naturally only deepened Floretta's pain, for she could not bear to be away from the forest for very long. To regain peace of mind, she needed to be alone and free in the forest, wandering at random and allowing her thoughts to wander too. And so, at length, she realised she would have to go out, even if it meant disobeying Grandmother.

That day, she completed her chores at great speed and then announced, attempting to suppress a tremor from her voice and hoping to appear casual: "I'm just going out for a little walk now." And she had reached the door before Grandmother objected; it seemed that Floretta's decisiveness had quite taken her aback.

"So early?" was all Grandmother could find to say, at last managing to add as Floretta lifted the bar, "You can't have got through all your chores yet… And, in any case, I'd rather you didn't go!"

Floretta had of course expected some objection, but even now when it came, the tone in Grandmother's voice surprised her; usually gently persuasive it was, for once, peremptory. Then she realised it was the first time she had ever been at variance with her; usually unquestioningly obedient, she had now developed a will of her own. Was this the dubious effect of exposure to the World of Man?

Very quietly she said, "I understand why you don't want me to go out, but I'm going. I cannot stay indoors like this forever, and I will be careful. After all, if anyone really did want to kidnap me, they could easily break in. The forest provides much more of an obstacle than these four walls." She concluded swiftly: "I don't want to cause you anxiety. I'll try not to be too long." And, before Grandmother could move to restrain her, she was gone.

* * * * *

Oh, what bliss to be in the fresh air and among the trees again, and on such a beautiful day! Almost at once, Floretta could feel her melancholy begin to lift. Her spirits rose and her heart seemed to soar up and along through the tops of the trees. She left the path and set off into a dense part of the forest where she could be sure to chance upon no one. For her, a child of the forest, the way was easy. As she walked, the forest began to whisper. At first the murmuring was just a rustle of leaves but then the meaning became clear: "Here at last is our little one. How tired she looks and how sad. How heavy she is finding the troubles of the world…"

Floretta was indeed tired. She found a seat on a mossy bank.

"Before, in her innocence, our little one considered life a straightforward affair… But now her innocence is past; she has witnessed just a little of the wickedness of humankind; she now views life through different eyes, eyes wiser but sadder…"

Floretta sighed. "I am not wise. Would that I were… I feel only that as I emerge into the World of Man my stupidity will betray me. I have been visited by the fear that I might do wrong without at once being aware of it…"

"You need not worry yourself so," replied the forest. "Great knowledge is no prerequisite for goodness. This is not to say that you are incapable of doing wrong, little one; you would be quite capable. You are no longer innocent, you are aware now of the existence of evil; you could decide to turn towards it away from the pursuit of goodness. But this would have to be a conscious decision and you would be fully aware of the change in yourself."

"Your words offer me some consolation," breathed Floretta, "for it occurred to me that if other humans were conscious of the pain and misery they were causing others, then surely they would be unable to commit these acts. And so I concluded that they might well be unaware of their own wickedness and that, in the same way, I might be unaware of mine…"

"You criticise yourself too much, dear child. Do not doubt yourself, should you fail to please others or fail to gain approval for doing what you believe is right. In the pursuit of goodness, it is necessary not merely to conform to the wishes of others by performing kindly deeds but also to act in ways which displease or even annoy others. What others may dub 'awkwardness' may well be a fine moral strength and therefore neither to be regretted nor shirked…

"But you have shown that you know this. You were assailed by powerful temptations and were not swayed one hair's breadth. Considerable scope for personal aggrandisement was placed within your grasp: great riches, grandeur, luxury, ease – by all of which people set great store – high rank, authority, a degree of power… All these could have been yours – in return for promises of love casually and spuriously given. But greed achieved no inroad on your character; appeals to deceit remained unheard…

"You responded well, though not – you may tell yourself – through moral choice, more through the mental confusion of the moment. But on future occasions, should similar opportunities present themselves, you will be aware of the choice before you; the decision – between good and evil – will be consciously made and all your own…

"And so it is good that we have exchanged ideas today, little one. In your life you will face trials far greater than you yet imagine. Though we seek to delay this we are powerless to prevent it forever. We can only hope that, when the time comes, you will feel that you are prepared…"

* * * * *

Even after the trees had become still and the forest voices had died away, Floretta remained sitting deep in thought upon the mossy bank. So lost had she been in her reveries that she could now no longer distinguish her ideas from those of the forest. The forest was now so silent that it seemed almost that there had been no voices, that the words had been all her own. For there had been almost nothing new; everything that had passed between her and the forest she had known in her heart already; the ideas had merely required expression and clarification.

Indeed, things she wished to know and could not guess at, the truth behind Grandmother's curious contradictions of her own identity, these matters had not even been touched upon. To resolve that paradox, she would clearly have to ask Grandmother herself. But should she? Thoughts of her grandmother brought an awareness of how long she had been absent and she wished she were at home offering reassurance. As she wished it, the wind blew again and once more the leaves began to chatter, though now incoherently. She stood to go and the wind took her up and began to speed her homewards. She ran and danced along, the weight of unshared problems now lifted, and began to feel light and happy.

She reached the clearing and skipped across towards the cottage, but as she approached her home she became abruptly aware of a difference. She stopped. From within came the unaccustomed sound of conversation. She listened. Voices had to mean people: men and women; visitors.

Visitors? But for what reason? The reason could be good... or it could mean that something was wrong.

Voices. People, talking loudly. But who?

CHAPTER 9

As Floretta stood before the cottage, a range of possibilities flashed across her mind. Most likely, she supposed, the visitors had been sent by one of the foreign merchants. It was possibly even the two men she had already had dealings with. Or else they had come from the Royal Palace, to ask for her hand again or even – more likely – to seize her and take her by force! She felt an impulse of panic as this last possibility occurred to her but suppressed it immediately, took herself in hand and attempted to appraise the situation.

If they were here on underhand business, how strange, she thought, that they had come on foot: glancing around, she could see no horses tethered. And indeed, if the visitors were kidnappers, surely they would not be advertising their presence so readily? They appeared to be making no attempt to muffle their voices or conceal their presence as she supposed villains might. She began to doubt her original supposition: had the visitors been intent on kidnap, they would surely have silenced Grandmother by now and, finding Floretta absent from the cottage, would have hidden themselves somewhere round about and have been lying in wait. They would doubtless have seized her by now.

Furthermore, Grandmother would never have unbarred the door for anyone even remotely suspicious: to Floretta's eyes, the door did not appear to have been forced; it bore no signs of battery. And equally, the forest would have warned her if there were any pressing danger. So the visitors could only be well-wishers. Who then? she asked herself. Why, how about the kindly pedlar? Had he not expressed a desire that they would meet again? But his noisy donkey cart was nowhere in evidence. In any case, how would he, or anyone else for that matter, have discovered the whereabouts of her home?

Overcoming her worst fears, Floretta moved up close to the window and peeped in. She saw Grandmother engaged in hearty conversation with two peasants – a man and a woman. Floretta was not aware of ever having seen them before but was relieved to observe Grandmother very much at her ease. And so, ever more curious, Floretta no longer hesitated but approached the door. As she entered, all eyes fell upon her and examined her, and she became aware that the couple had someone else with them, a young girl of approximately her own age or perhaps a little older.

Grandmother beamed at Floretta. "We've been wondering when you would decide to come home," she said and then, addressing her visitors, announced, "Well, this is the pride of my life, my own Floretta!"

"Very nice to meet you, Miss," grinned the man.

"These good people are our nearest neighbours," explained Grandmother. "They live about four miles off along this side of the ridge in the direction of the river, a bit more towards town than us. They thought it would only be neighbourly to look us up while this fine weather lasted."

Floretta smiled shyly. She joined the group and took up a kneeling position on the floor, all the chairs for once being taken. Feeling she should say something she remarked: "Yes, weather like this draws everyone out of doors."

"Aye, we don't normally get out much," agreed the peasant woman. "So we don't meet all that many folk. After all, four mile here and four mile back too often is a bit far just to 'pass by' as they say." She laughed a funny cackle of a laugh.

"Aye, that it is," agreed her husband.

"We've been telling your mother," the woman still addressed Floretta, "how well she is looking. I've been wondering what her secret is." Floretta became suddenly rather more alert. "I told her too – curious it was – how we happened to meet your old grandmother out in the forest – must be years ago now – and how I'd swear as she told us as your mother – what is sitting here so live and well before you now – had gone and died!" The woman broke into laughter and Grandmother laughed too and then all the circle laughed except Floretta, who sat quietly, her ears burning, most anxious to learn more, but concealing her anxiety and smiling politely.

"Aye, the old woman told us how sad she had been when her daughter passed on, years before, she said. Most distressed we were to hear the news. And, you know, it was her all right no mistake and not just someone else's old mother, and she said the name clear enough: Flora."

"Aye." Now the man spoke up. "But she was that old, May, wasn't she now, and not quite with us. Her mind must ha' been going. She didn't know lies from truth no more."

"No, I suppose not, poor dear, rest her soul."

"Aye, rest her soul," he echoed.

"That's part the reason we've come," said the woman. "I'll admit it. We were curious, nosey if you like. We've met other folk as were sure you were gone, Flora, and when we heard from the same folk as you'd appeared live and well at market, well, we thought we could only come and see for ourselves. Some even reckoned you'd come back from the dead and said as they were scared to greet you in case! Now, I ask you! But it does go to show how out of touch we've got. Should ha' come before, I know, right unneighbourly we've been – I'll admit that too."

"Well, so have we, I suppose, if it comes to that," said Grandmother.

"Maybe, but two wrongs don't make a right," asserted the peasant man somewhat irrelevantly, and then, slapping his knee, said, "But you tell me, Flora, what's your secret, you've kept so young. I'll warrant you're same age at least as my old wife here but you don't look it!"

"Harry Walder! I like that!" objected his wife.

"Well, it's true, love, you said it yourself. I don't say you're badly kept but Flora here, well, there's no comparison."

Grandmother smiled: "You keep asking for my secret. Well, I haven't really got one. Though maybe there's something in this: I've led a peaceful solitary life, alone with Nature except for the blessing of a gentle child…" Floretta lowered her eyes demurely, almost embarrassed, unaccustomed to being the subject of conversation. Grandmother continued: "And I never really died, I can assure you, not even for one moment."

The peasants seemed unable to furnish a jocular reply in the face of such seriousness, and so the gathering fell temporarily silent. When conversation revived, strangely it was the couple's quiet and rather plain daughter who initiated its revival. "Funny isn't it," she remarked, "what strange rumours get round. You can never believe what you hear these days. But did you hear that story about the Prince? Prince Elbert, that is? Not the one about his… you know…" She blushed. "The other one… Well, rumour has it he proposed to a peasant girl – rumour don't say who though – in the market place it was, and rumour reckons she turned him down, right there before the crowd!"

"We have heard that story," answered Grandmother rather coldly.

"Have you? I bet you were amazed. I was. I reckon as she hadn't heard that Julien was betrothed and fancied that if Elbert would have her, so might the Crown Prince himself. Well, she's missed her chance. I can't believe anyone could refuse him though, can you? Elbert, I mean… So handsome and so rich? My, the stories that get round, can't know whether to believe it or not…"

"Aye, you can't trust rumour," remarked her father as if anxious to conclude the matter.

"There's another rumour that got me thinking," continued the girl nonetheless, "and that was… that the girl as Elbert proposed to…"

"Look, watch your tongue!" interrupted her father. "You little gossip! I've told you before!"

"Go on, Julia, what did you hear?" prompted Grandmother with a politeness and composure that astounded Floretta who herself was quite speechless.

Despite the obvious discomfort of her parents, the girl went on: "Well, it sounded from the descriptions of the girl as have been going round… that it could only be your daughter Floretta here."

"You shouldn't have said it!" pounced her mother. "No," she told Floretta. "Julia's wrong. Rumours don't say it's you at all, dear. It just occurred that it might be, that's all, when we saw how pretty you've become. Take no notice of this little hussy of ours. She shouldn't go spreading stories around – we've warned her not to."

"Why not?" Floretta heard herself speaking. "Why shouldn't she say it, if it's true?"

"I told you, Mother!" chirped Julia, victorious, but to her disappointment all eyes were on Floretta, not her.

"It's true," said Floretta. "I did refuse His Highness the Prince Elbert. I'd never met him before, I felt no love for him, and so I felt I could not at that time arrange to marry him. His palace meant nothing to me, I didn't even think of it. All I thought of was the happy life I would be leaving here with…" She broke off suddenly and lowered her head, biting her lip to avoid the tell-tale word 'Grandmother'. The group continued staring stonily at her, but she had no more to say.

"Well," commented Julia in a joking voice, making a further bid for attention. "It's all right for some people. It's only too easy to say riches mean nothing when you're blessed with looks and can afford to take your pick…"

Floretta felt hurt, and somehow blameworthy, though mystified as to why she should, as once again this unfair accusation of conceit was hurled at her. She was too pleasant and polite by far to retaliate with accusations of spite – though they would have been perfectly warranted – but, fortunately perhaps, did not need to: the girl's parents did it for her.

Her mother: "Oh, be quiet. You're only jealous. You little mischief-maker…"

Her father: "Aye, if you can't be nicer, we'll leave you at home next time." Trying to smooth things over, he pretended it was a joke and winked at Floretta.

Grandmother took the opportunity of this break in the conversation to offer her visitors some refreshment, after which they politely took their leave. But before they left, the peasant man felt there was something important he had to say. "You, young lady," he told Floretta, "seemed not one bit worried by what you did the other day. Do you know what you've done? I think you need to know the whole town has been talking about it, and they say the Royal Household is not pleased. I've heard it said that, if they knew where to find the girl, well… A stranger, they say, thank goodness. So next time, if there is a next time, anyone asks if it was you, just you deny it, just you play innocent. You're lucky, we won't let on, we'll deny it for you if we hear your name mentioned again. But, well… I just thought I should warn you…"

The women moved the conversation on to more mundane topics and, after exchanging a few lighter pleasantries, the family left.

CHAPTER 10

Floretta feared the morrow would bring more visitors and perhaps further disturbances, but to her relief none came. The next day, and then others after it, passed quietly, the two women absorbed in their daily tasks and content with their own thoughts. They shared little conversation but there was peace between them; the silence did not hang heavy.

Floretta wondered greatly at the words of the peasants, at the meaning of their warning to her, but wondered perhaps even more at Grandmother's words. But she asked no questions of Grandmother for, she now realised, the questions were there already in the air, though they remained unspoken, and would surely be answered all in good time when Grandmother felt so disposed and certainly, she felt sure, not before. Furthermore, Grandmother now caused Floretta much less concern for, despite the disturbing rumours that had been passed on to them, she grew daily more relaxed and was now less troubled about allowing Floretta outside the cottage.

When Floretta entered Grandmother's bedroom one morning to find her tending the iridescent flower which stood as ever in its pot on the window sill, she could sense that something of great consequence was in the air. For usually, Grandmother showed little or no interest in the flower; the task of tending it had fallen to Floretta, which was really just as Floretta wanted, for she adored the flower. She had cherished it, coaxed it, whispered little endearments to it whenever tending it for many months now, and the plant had responded with a healthy growth.

So, to find Grandmother for once addressing the flower instead of ignoring it came not so much as a surprise to Floretta (for she had always suspected that Grandmother did speak to the flower, if in secret) but as a sign that the momentous disclosure she had been awaiting must be due. For, as Floretta entered the room, Grandmother did not hurriedly pretend to be otherwise occupied but turned to her and smiled and called to her, "Come and see the flower, Floretta."

Floretta went across. "Look at the leaves," Grandmother said to her. "How strong and well formed they are, and the petals, how soft and delicate and yet so firm. Touch the petals, Floretta, feel, they are as soft as the wings of a butterfly. How well you have cared for this flower."

Floretta modestly lowered her head before this praise; yet she knew it was true – she had cared for it well – and in turn it had cared for them. This was something she longed to say aloud. Dared she say it? Scarcely had the words formed on her lips before she heard them emerge: "Yes," she heard herself say. "And the flower has repaid my care. It has brought us good health."

"Yes, Floretta, that is correct. What a perceptive child you are. Your good health is natural to you, for you are young, but mine, mine has all sprung from this flower. Did you realise, I would have died that awful morning many months ago now, but for the activity of this lovely flower? It captured the small flame of my spirit when I was on the point of death and bade it stay a little longer in that frail body. And that small flame of my spirit still lives today, and now lives easily in this strong youthful body."

"So then, you are Grandmother?"

"Yes, I am, but these lips have told no lies even though their words have baffled you. For also living in this body, and growing daily ever stronger, is the spirit of Flora, my daughter and your mother."

Floretta gasped in wonder. "How can this be?" she breathed.

"I will explain. When this flower came to us, it carried with it the spirit of the young Flora lost in the woods. And right from the start, her spirit began to leave the flower, joining my weak spirit in my old body and strengthening it. As Flora's spirit entered my body, she gradually brought it youth again."

"So your body contains two spirits," said Floretta. "You are both there. I am talking to you both… But do you never conflict? Is not one spirit stronger?"

"The spirit of Flora is stronger, but she does not dominate. Speaking to you now is your old grandmother, who feels only gratitude to the vigorous soul which has joined her. You see, but for Flora's life strength – her spiritual life strength – I would have died that day. Do not doubt how close I was to death, Floretta. No one, no doctor, no surgeon, could have saved me. At first, I was not aware that it was my daughter's life strength which was healing my body and allowing it to live, but gradually, as I began to realise the truth, I opened my heart wide and welcomed her.

"We kept all this secret from you for, to be sure, if we had spoken of the magic before it was complete, we might well have broken the spell. I have never been sure whether this belief sprang from truth or superstition, but we had no wish to gamble with so high a stake. We have been waiting for today, for at last the change is complete. This body cannot grow any younger. It stands before you now as the body of Flora, your mother, just as she was before she died. In fact, this body is your mother; it is no longer my body. So far, we have found it useful that our two souls are joined – we can benefit from the wisdom and experience of age without sacrificing the energy of youth."

"That will be why," observed Floretta, "you have several times recently amazed me with your presence of mind… But now, it seems, I have a problem. How then should I address you? Should I still call you Grandmother?"

"That will be for you to decide. We will not be offended which of us you choose to address."

Floretta reflected. "I have never known my mother," she decided, "but I should like to call you Mother. For it seems most inappropriate to address someone as young as yourself as 'Grandmother' merely by habit. And I feel it would be safer, now that locally you are becoming known as my mother."

"Exactly so. If we appear to contradict ourselves too much, I fear only trouble will come of it."

Floretta's fears were here so accurately expressed for her that she could add nothing. A brief shadow passed across her mind, marring for one moment her joy. She did not allow it to dwell but moved her thoughts quickly on. "What of the flower?" she asked. "How does it feel now that Mother's spirit has left it? Has it lost the power of speech?"

"Let me reassure you that I have not, Floretta," answered the flower. "Even though Flora has left me, I am not powerless. I can still speak, and indeed there is much that I want to say, so much is there for me to acknowledge and to praise… You see, though originally I thrived on the power of Flora's goodness, now I thrive on yours. Having sprung from a human source, I need a human element to sustain me, and now that Flora's energy is employed in producing and sustaining physical form, I have needed to look elsewhere for energy and have found what I suspected – there seems no end to the power of goodness which emanates from your heart."

* * * * *

Later that day, Floretta returned to the flower to pose a further question that was troubling her. "Tell me one more thing, dear flower.

How did you first come into being? What happened to create such a wonderful bloom as you? Or do you not know?"

"Certainly I know, little one, but have you not realised? I will tell you. I was the expression of a goodness, a life force that could not die. Many years ago now, when Flora collapsed numbed with cold into a forest ravine, physically she died. But she was not entirely dead, and as her body decayed and merged with the soil of the forest and became covered by layers, and then more layers, of leaves, and as all trace of her became hidden in a rich leafy mould, a flower began to grow, springing from her heart, and then, one fine spring morning, shooting to the light of day. I was that flower.

"For years I grew there alone, unseen and untouched, the forest my sole companion, longing to see you again, thinking only of the day when we would be reunited. That day came. When you saw me, you took me for a flower, and you were right – I am a flower. It did not occur to you that I might be your mother. I yearned to tell you but dared not and thankfully you did not ask: it was unnecessary for you to question what I was and likewise you saw no reason to question 'who?'.

"Now you know that I did indeed possess identity, you know who I was, that I was Flora. You also know that I am no longer Flora. Who am I now, you might ask? I am no one. And what am I now? Now I am only a flower, just a flower."

CHAPTER 11

The flower asked to be moved from the window sill in Grandmother's bedroom where it had remained for months now to a more central position from which it might see more of them both. So Floretta carried the pot through into the living room and placed it on the window sill there, positioning it carefully at the end nearest her room, so that, providing she left her door ajar, she would be able to look up and see the flower during the night.

That day was a happy one; there were no longer any secrets between the three and conversation was free-flowing and relaxed. Floretta was unusually talkative, not only in the house as she completed her chores but most especially when she went out later into the forest; she had so much to tell the trees. So, with little divergence from routine, passed the happiest day Floretta had spent for many months since Grandmother had originally fallen ill and Floretta had first brought the flower to the cottage. Life now seemed without problem or paradox.

The next day and the one after were days of idyllic peace. Each morning when she was awakened by the bright sunrays which slanted in through her bedroom window, Floretta would look up and smile with joy to see once more her lovely flower standing there, its glorious iridescent petals outlined with the bright gold of the morning sun. Thus the day would begin on a note of perfect happiness. And so it would continue; frequently as she worked, Floretta would pause to cast a loving glance upon her flower or to look beyond it through the window at the beautiful forest trees, green and fresh still with their early summer leaves.

But one afternoon, as she turned to gaze upon the flower and beyond, she was moved not to an emotion of adoration and love but to a reaction of alarm. Standing outside, his face pushed close to the glass, attempting to peer in, was someone… someone… She searched her memory but could not be sure who. But, whoever it was, she felt he was not welcome. His features were so familiar she knew at once she had met him recently. Yet still she could not place him; she could recall merely that their meeting had not been a pleasant one.

"Mother!" she called urgently when at last she recovered from the initial shock.

"What is it?" came the reply, and quickly, young beautiful Flora – who now looked scarcely more than a few years senior to Floretta – strode purposefully through from the adjoining room. Though looking so youthful and so fresh, now that the changes in her were completed and she had reached an equilibrium, she was possessed somehow of a great maturity and calm.

"My goodness!" she remarked as her eyes fell upon the face at the window. "No wonder you sounded alarmed, Floretta! How strange that he of all people should visit us! What can he want? Well, I suppose we had better let him in: if he is intent on entry, we would not succeed in keeping him out for long."

The door was not locked. Without hesitation Flora lifted the latch. As the door fell open, in stepped their uninvited guest whom Floretta now recognised as that very scoundrel who had attempted to sell them 'protection' on market day.

He bowed elaborately, doffing his gaily plumed hat. "Good day, my ladies," he said. "Elavisado once more at your service."

"Indeed," replied Flora. "And what are you selling this time, I wonder? As you can see we lack nothing."

"Good lady, I fancied such would be your reply, but I trust you are not serious. For, if you are so badly informed as to believe yourselves genuinely without need, then you show yourselves to be even more requiring of my assistance than I had imagined. If I shared your opinion on this matter, would I have devoted these last weeks to seeking the whereabouts of your good residence here? No. So hear me out, for I know you have much to gain from me, or, perhaps I should say rather more realistically, you have much to lose, should you not avail yourselves of my offer of assistance."

"Well Sir, it seems you have greater concern for us than we have ourselves, though for what reason I cannot imagine. But I suspect your interest will wane when you learn we have nothing to offer as payment for your services; as yet we have finished no more shirts."

He appeared offended. "Would I spend so long tracing you merely to acquire the price of a shirt? As always you misjudge me. You accuse me of self-interest; you imply that I have come not to help you but merely to profit from you. Ladies, you do me wrong. You are mistaken."

"I suspect not," replied Flora.

With a grave expression, he looked deep into Flora's face, as if questioning whether the slight he felt was really intended, his sad dark eyes protesting innocence. Then he turned and instead looked closely upon Floretta.

"As I look upon your lovely daughter," he began haltingly, addressing Flora, yet not averting his gaze from Floretta. "As I look upon her, I see the danger of loving her, for she could not be mine. And yet I feel myself irresistibly drawn as must so many others have been… drawn, before."

For one instant Floretta began to wonder if he really was sincere, only to dismiss this thought as he continued his bargaining:

"And so the reward I ask for the services I can offer (services which incidentally I have already begun providing) is minimal, considering the gain to you and the expense to myself… My price is low, as I find it a pleasure to be of assistance to such gentle women."

"In what way have you already begun providing us with a service?" countered Flora laughingly. "I see no way in which we have yet benefited from your presence."

"Ah!" he replied. "It is not by my presence you benefit but by the activities to which I devote my time when I am not here! So smooth is my tongue, so subtle are my devices that I can arrange against great odds for you to remain anonymous; I can arrange for the location of your dwelling to remain a secret (few know of your true identity but me); I can arrange, if you wish, for word to circulate that the rumours spreading about you are fictitious, invented by ill-wishers to the Crown, exaggerated by importunate fools, dreamed by the fanciful… I can arrange all this, weaving a web of new reality, carefully extinguishing all breath of the old one, carefully silencing all who would breathe to the contrary… I can arrange… in short, I can arrange… anything. Any means of protecting your privacy, of securing your safety, which you would find personally satisfying, I can arrange it."

"Can you arrange for us to be protected from scoundrels such as yourself?" asked Flora pointedly.

Refusing to be baulked, he replied: "Of course, Madam, if my devices are adequate, no one will know of your whereabouts but me, so no one else will bother you."

"But why should others bother us?" asked Floretta rather artlessly in the circumstances, the troubles of a few weeks previous having merged into the past, the residual threat of danger having diminished by the day. "What are the rumours you speak of? Why should we need to conceal the situation of our cottage?"

"Ah, the rumours…" he murmured almost wistfully. "Have you no inkling of them? Can you not imagine? First I heard the story of a woman so fresh and lively she looked to be her own daughter's twin… I heard that this same woman could work miracles with her hands, that her craftswomanship surpassed that of the great seamstresses of a century gone by, that nothing to rival it would be found amongst the rich tapestries that adorn the walls of the Royal Palace…"

He leaned closer to Floretta and adopted a more confidential tone: "And I heard too other rumours, my dear… of a maiden possessed of such sumptuous beauty, she felt free to disdain the advances of a prince… of how this same beguiling creature claimed innocence when all who were discerning could see that the years of her experience were beyond the years of her face… I learned of how this same remarkable girl was the daughter of that same woman who held the Secret of Eternal Youth! That they sold shirts together in the market place, tendering garments so well formed that, by common consent, they could not have been fashioned by the coarse hands of peasant women, unless those hands possessed some means of sorcery…"

He paused, as if expecting some comment – a protest perhaps. When none came, he continued readily: "It was not long before I realised that I had of course made the acquaintance of those two women and that they were none other than you two standing here before me now. I remembered how you had spurned my own well-intentioned offer of protection, rather arrogantly I felt, and how I had been rather curious at the time as to how you intended to maintain your own security…

"And so it was that I came to connect you with another strange story of witchcraft, this story circulating the taverns and reported as having first sprung from the eager lips of two slaves – eunuchs originally from beyond the mountains – joyful at having been freed by the sudden death of their master in these parts and who delighted in recounting their tale repeatedly in great detail. I sought them out and heard it all again from their own lips: the wonders you had wrought and the great fear you had cast upon them at the time…

"For a while, I assumed quite naturally that the reason for your refusal of the protection I had offered was that you knew you could protect yourselves still better by your own spells. But then I realised that, of the many who spoke of you, I was one of the very few who had met you, one of the few who could judge you from first-hand knowledge…

"I pondered the matter for several days and at length decided that the impression of innocence and naïveté I had originally gained was a true one and that the reputation of guile that you had since achieved was the product of the muddled words of half-drunken idlers – those who love to exaggerate over their ale – originating from the fanciful inventions of those who had really only glimpsed the truth from the back of the crowd…

"So, eventually, without fear, realising that if you bore me ill you would have stricken me earlier (that is, if you were able) I decided to approach you again to offer my services." Having completed his speech, he bowed elegantly to offer his respect, and then stood awaiting a reply from them.

"Sir," began Flora, "that you speak the truth I do not challenge, and yet your conclusions I would dispute. I still aver that we do not need your help. The stories you tell do not surprise me, but still I feel we are in no danger. Before you, no one has disturbed us: there is nothing of value to be gained here, we possess no great riches to tempt the ambitious…"

"No one has come as yet," he interrupted. "But that does not mean they will not come. If the rumours are allowed to spread unchecked, it will not be long before others grow curious. And they may not be as well meaning as myself, bear that in mind. At present those who think of coming fear your powers and are restrained by caution, but soon there will come adventurers, happy to test the strength of their own spells. They will ignore tales of great beauty – such stories abound – but the lure of the Secret of Eternal Youth, that they will find irresistible… For this secret they will be prepared to face all perils."

"If they come, then they will come," replied Flora. "I have no way to stop them. If you wish to ward off ill-wishers by quashing the rumours, then you are at liberty to do so, and I can appreciate that we should feel grateful towards you for helping us in this way, but we can only thank you. As I have said, we are quite powerless to pay you; we have nothing of value to offer you. So you had best be on your way to do what you will."

But Elavisado was not keen to go. He bowed politely in recognition of Flora's closure of the interview but made no move to leave. "Madam," he requested. "Pray suffer my presence a little longer. I am glad that I have been able to convince you of your dangerous situation, of your need for caution, and I acknowledge your gratitude for what I have already achieved. But, if you will allow me, there is still one point on which I would like your agreement before I take my leave…"

"Very well," said Flora. "Make your point quickly."

"Well, Madam. You have agreed as to your debt to me, that you should reward me for what I have already done, even if you have no wish to employ me in the future…"

"Yes," she replied impatiently. "Continue quickly!"

"If I may remind you of what I have already done… In the taverns I have joined discussion about you and admitted acquaintance with you, always speaking in support of you… I have done much to dispel the aura of witchcraft surrounding your names… I have sounded out opinion and laid foundations for the solution of your problems… Why, with my soft persuasive words the town's gossipers would forget you, shrug their shoulders, dismiss their suspicions as false and move on to some fresh scandal, which I would provide! Indeed, I am resourceful enough…"

"You have said all this," said Flora, obviously tiring of the conversation again. "I thought there was more."

"Madam, there is," he insisted. "For I am attempting to show you how you may repay your debt to me." And yet still he could not make his point but persisted in hedging around it. "Good lady," he continued. "I can see too well that you are no witch – I have met others who were, and you lack their mark. You are not possessed of secret powers. But I can also see by your radiance, your glowing health, that you conceal someone, or something, which does have power. Why, the whole cottage possesses this same glow which surrounds you and your daughter! As I look around me now I notice how the order and charm of your home surpasses by far that of any ordinary household. Look! Even the flower on your window sill is resplendent with this wonderful glow of perfect health!"

At the mention of the flower Floretta started. So he had noticed it! Her mother, thank goodness, seemed quite unperturbed. "At last we have it," she was saying. "You seek to obtain this glow of perfect health for yourself."

"But of course, I admit as much," came his reply. He now sounded rather less friendly. "I admit that part of my motive is personal gain. I cannot afford to be completely altruistic in my daily affairs. And you did inquire how you could repay me…"

"I did not," Flora corrected him.

"Well, I offer an honest service. Protection is my business," he answered almost menacingly, while Floretta grew increasingly afraid of him. "My reputation is good, so trust me. Use your sense, Madam, share your secret with me lest you lose it for yourselves!"

"In return for a secret we cannot give," argued Flora, "you offer us guile, which we like not! Your service is not honest and therefore we can share nothing with you. You were not frank with us; you disprove your own case. Our health is the mark of simple honest living, of satisfaction with our lives as they are. You cannot share such health, for you could never share our way of life!"

Floretta stood petrified across the room as the two stood contemplating each other, their business still not completed. Would he never go? thought Floretta – he had far outstayed his welcome – and how could her mother dare stand up to him the way she did?

"All we can offer you," continued Flora calmly, "in return for what you may have done to help us, is refreshment before you continue on your way. Floretta, bring some tumblers from the scullery, will you please! Sir, accept our hospitality for I assure you there is naught else to be gained from us."

But before Floretta could reach the scullery, Elavisado had made a quick move to the door. "I will not trouble you for refreshment, thank you, Madam," he said almost breathlessly, now appearing to be in a hurry. "A small memento from you would have sufficed as payment. Perhaps a lock of your daughter's lovely hair, or a petal from this remarkable flower…"

He stood beside the doorway, one hand reaching for the latch and the other stretching out towards the flower. Floretta gasped and stepped forward. She must protect the flower!

"Do not touch the flower!" she begged. "I would gladly give a hundred locks of my hair if you will spare my flower. I have cherished it so…" Too late she realised her folly: he had tricked her into acknowledging its importance. A triumphant grin was spreading across his face.

"Come, come, Floretta," her mother scolded, trying to distract attention from the flower. "Surely you are not serious. Your hair is of more value…" But her voice quavered as she spoke and her words missed their desired effect. She moved steadily across the room towards the window and the flower but before she could reach it, Elavisado had stretched out his hand and touched it.

"Touch those petals and you will surely die!" cried Flora suddenly, as if impelled by some will other than her own.

A look of fear passed across his face, his hand trembled and hesitated. But then, as if wishing not to be completely outdone, with one deft movement he plucked a leaf from the plant and a second later was gone from the cottage. The pot trembled slightly but did not fall over. Then the hooves of the vagabond's horse were heard in hasty departure.

"We have won," sighed Floretta with relief. "The flower is safe. It will not miss one leaf."

"Maybe," replied Flora. "But, I fear he has taken away its secret."

CHAPTER 12

The confrontation with Elavisado had proved much more of an ordeal for Flora than had been apparent at the time. Though having preserved such a dignified mien throughout, Flora was now distraught. "Would that we had never gone to the market in Torquella," she told Floretta woefully. "It was your grandmother who wanted so much to go, and never I. She hankered after it so much I decided to take her that one more time – for her sake. I am content in the forest and have never cared much for the town, and would as lief not have gone… Had I but known how times had deteriorated, I would have stayed away…

"Seeing old friends is quite pleasant, I know," she went on, "though I can manage without it. And I can cope with love-struck princes, I suppose, but duplicitous scoundrels and murderous slave traders are too much for me…"

Floretta felt sad to see her mother so distressed and did everything she could to reassure her, though she in turn had her own regrets – which she kept to herself. In her heart, she regretted her lack of reserve at the crucial moment, reproached herself for the outburst which had revealed her unusual attachment to the flower. She vowed never to lose control of herself in such a situation again and determined to take as an example to herself the presence of mind, strength and courage her mother had at the time displayed.

Had Elavisado realised the full significance of the flower, she wondered, or had he merely admired its brilliance and colour? She had no way of knowing, but grieved nonetheless; she feared not only for the flower but for the life and health of her mother which she knew to spring from it. Worry for herself did not enter into the equation, however; she did not see herself as being affected, or as having importance. And yet time is a great healer. Several peaceful weeks passed after Elavisado's disagreeable intrusion, and life at the little cottage settled once more into a gentle rhythm.

The day was fine and breezy; warm sunlight flickered down through the gently rocking branches, playing tricks of shifting light and shade with the patterned barks of the trees; the sound of happy birdsong filled the air as the young birds played together and practised their flying up high between the branches nearest sun and sky. It was as if all Nature were contented and on such days Flora and Floretta were contented too.

As mother and daughter, Flora and Floretta, wandered on at their leisure through the sunny forest in search of early ripe berries, Floretta felt her last fears disperse. Elavisado. Goodness, he was a cunning fellow! Obviously trying to obtain a payment for no service rendered! He had a persuasive tongue and he knew it. But there was no foundation to his reasoning: no one else had ventured forth to annoy them: they had no need for 'protection'. Why, their 'dangerous situation' was but a figment of his crafty imagination! There was indeed no cause for concern, for, as Floretta had predicted, the flower did not appear to have suffered from the loss of a leaf; it had made no complaints, and had even produced a tender little bud of new leaves at the spot from which the leaf had been so rudely plucked.

The two women turned at last to return to their cottage, their bark baskets only partially full of wild hindberries, few as yet having ripened. They strolled happily amongst the trees, the gentle whispering of the leaves and the cheerful singing of the birds pleasant upon their ears.

Gradually they became aware of another sound mingling with the forest murmurings. Yes, it was the sound of human discourse. How unusual in this region of the forest! As the two moved on in the direction of their home, the voices grew increasingly loud and clear. Quickening their step, they drew near the clearing around the cottage. But they did not emerge from the cover of the trees, for confronting them was an alarming scene: a dozen or more horsemen, some still on horseback but some dismounting, were spaced about the cottage, intent upon watching it, but seemingly wary of approaching it, maintaining instead a discreet distance.

With care not to reveal themselves, Flora and Floretta drew closer still, curious to discover the purpose of this group. Snatches of the conversation now reached their ears:

"…escape with our lives while we can…"

"…no ordinary cottage…"

"…don't like it at all…"

"…unusual for such a silence to be cast over a place…"

It was true, Flora and Floretta then noticed, the birds had now stopped singing and the trees were still.

"…peasant cottages usually full of life…"

"…no hens…"

It was no surprise to Floretta that their hens had taken themselves off to hide somewhere in the forest or behind the house: they were not used to so many strangers. But the horsemen were right: an uncanny silence hung over the scene, so that their voices seemed to echo back and forth across the clearing. As they surveyed the cottage, they stood in the main with their backs to the two women, and so the two were able to creep up still nearer under the cover of the trees.

"Whatever you say, they must be inside…"

"And they won't be coming out to greet us…"

"How can you feel so sure?"

"Well, they won't come out before they're ready…"

"Most like, they're hiding away preparing spells to cast over us…"

"I think they might well be out here already… Can you not feel the chill?"

"The chill? They're here as spirits you mean…"

"…mingling with us but all the time invisible?.."

"The thought is not amusing…"

"Be silent, you superstitious fools!" This loud harsh voice could be heard with no difficulty. "If you can contribute nothing but poltroonery and dissension then be gone! We have no need of you! Those who are steadfast and remain will share your reward!"

This gaily attired cavalier was conspicuous as the leader of the group, the others wearing the comparatively restrained blue and gold of the King's Guard. A bold fellow, he had dismounted and taken a few steps towards the cottage. The others showed no sign of following, and so he turned to face them. As he did so, his gaze fell momentarily in the direction of the two women, who feared immediately that they might have been seen. With relief they realised they had not, and with this realisation came another: having now seen the full face of the cavalier, they had recognised him as none other than Elavisado! What cunning scheme had prompted that shameless scoundrel to return to their lonely and humble dwelling?

"I tell you, I've been inside," he was saying, "and there is nothing to be feared from the two who live there! Otherwise, how would I have escaped when I came before?"

"There may be others you have not seen…"

"I say you escaped before with a poisoned tongue…" remarked one large older fellow icily, slumped astride his horse like someone weary of too many campaigns. "You've done naught but revile us since we left…"

"Methinks he's afraid. His fear has robbed him of his smooth tongue…"

"Aye," rejoined another. "And if the mission is so easy, how is it he did not accomplish it before on his own?"

"Just so," agreed the first fellow. "Why should he need a dozen of the King's best men before daring to venture again into these parts?"

"Witchcraft is the answer." A younger soldier spoke up now. "We all know it, and I can feel it."

"Cast off your superstition, you fool!" cried Elavisado. "Or you are undone!"

"But are we not here on a superstitious errand?" remarked the veteran. "Why else have we come?"

Elavisado was seen to maintain his sangfroid only with something of an effort. "I will ask you not to question our presence here," he replied bitingly, "nor still to question my authority. You will remember only that you are here under my command on a mission for your Crown Prince and that the King's life and the security of the Throne are at stake."

"Aye, but we remember too that you're not our Colonel," the veteran retorted. "This mission would have been a different matter entirely if he'd been assigned the charge. We'll complete the business, but only for the sake of our king. We'll show you no allegiance."

Elavisado could not have been pleased by these remarks but chose to ignore them. "Now, if we may consider these two women," he resumed. "They may well be witches but, if they are, their powers are minimal. We have nothing to fear, provided we avoid their noxious liquids, as you have already been warned. They sought to poison me when I came before, if you will remember, but were quite powerless when I refused to drink! So, let us go quickly about our task…"

The veteran dismounted and, as if this were a sign, those who still vacillated and remained on horseback followed suit.

"Indeed," Elavisado told them, "it is fortunate that we come at a time when the two are absent, for even though, as I say, their powers are limited, it is best not to incur their wrath. If they have not seen us, they can fashion no dolls. And, of course, were they present, they might work some quick spell to divert the power of their talisman. We can congratulate ourselves on our timely arrival: the women are away. For we do not need them, we want nothing of them. Merely the power that sustains them…"

Having at last mustered their courage, the group stealthily approached the cottage, still wary, as if half believing they would find the two women lying in wait.

"Are you sure it is merely the plant you speak of which we need take?" asked the veteran. "Perhaps they were misleading you. Should we not use this opportunity to search for some more usual amulet?"

At the mention of the plant, Floretta stiffened; there was no question as to which plant they were referring to. She could not let them touch it! Better that they take her! She felt her mother's hand close about her wrist, as if she had sensed her exact thoughts.

"It is without the slightest doubt the plant that we need," Elavisado was saying. "You have seen the leaf and cannot demur. With your own eyes you have all seen the intense vigour which has not forsaken it during these days it has been mine! Even in my pocket it has not crumbled. And, I promise you, when you see the plant you will appreciate its influence. It is amazing! If it were at the window as before, you would have seen it already and understood at once. They have moved it – prudent of them, unusually so – but it will not prove hard to find. Forward! Let us enter quickly and take possession."

Elavisado gingerly lifted the latch and entered first. The others followed one by one. One young soldier was to remain outside to guard the horses but, on hearing gasps from within, he left his post and rushed to see what wonder could have elicited this reaction from his cynical comrades. Before he could enter, Elavisado emerged, bearing aloft the glorious and glowing iridescent flower upon which all eyes were fixed. The others followed quickly behind, the last one carefully closing the door.

"Mother, I must stop them…" pleaded Floretta as she watched the guards collect their mounts again.

"No, my child, we can do nothing," Flora told her sadly.

But Floretta was not to be convinced. How could she just stand by? She cast aside her recent resolution for presence of mind in situations such as this. Wrenching herself free from her mother's grasp with unprecedented force, she rushed wildly forward as the horsemen gathered their reins in preparation for mounting.

"Stop! Stop!" she cried feebly. "You may not take my flower! You have no claim to it!"

"It's the girl! The little witch!" screamed the men, seized by a foolish panic which threatened to infect the horses.

"Ignore the child! She cannot harm you!" yelled Elavisado to no avail: the frightened horses scattered and the men seemed ready to scatter after them.

One young man found his horse would no longer allow him astride; the excited beast neighed and reared and then bolted, and the terrified young man was forced to jump up behind one of his fellows. These two set off immediately into the forest, ignoring the loss of the fine steed.

At this moment Floretta reached Elavisado as he too fought to discipline his beast. He seemed almost to be juggling, his hands overfull with the plant, the reins and his horsewhip. Floretta beat with her little fists at his heavily booted thigh and pounded on the flank of his stallion. "Leave my flower!" she sobbed. "Or its colours will dazzle you. Its, its scent will intoxicate you. Its, its power will undo you…"

Elavisado merely laughed. "What sweet curses, my pretty one!" he mocked. "See!" he shouted to his men. "She is merely a child. She is powerless. There is nothing to fear from her!"

Observing that the group were succeeding eventually in subduing their horses and that they would within seconds all be gone, Floretta made one last desperate bid to thwart Elavisado: she slid her hands under the leather side-strap of his saddle and held on tight. Even so, as if feeling not the least encumbrance, the horse set off under its master's prompting and began to gallop, pulling Floretta alongside at such speed that her slim legs could not prevent themselves from dragging behind, the skin of her knees protected from the rough path only by her thick skirts. Indeed, her body trailed so close to the horse's pounding hooves that she was in grave danger of being impaled under them. Elavisado whipped his horse so that they gained even more speed. But still Floretta did not let go.

"Leave go, you witch," he cursed, "or may the devil take you!" The horse could go no faster, so Elavisado turned his whip instead upon Floretta. Its stinging bite fell across her face and arms, but she held on, scarcely thinking, but vaguely determined that he would not get away without her; she would at least cause him to lose hold of the flower; she would try to dismount him.

Now he turned his heavy spurred boot upon her. "Curse you!" he fumed as he kicked out. He kicked at her tender hands, but they did not flinch. He kicked with his thick heel at her shoulder, but still she bore the pain. Then a savage blow met the side of her head and, in the blackness which followed, Floretta knew not whether she still held on.

CHAPTER 13

When Floretta regained consciousness, her first awareness was of the pain which throbbed in her swollen hands and then of the soreness which covered her whole body. As she collected her thoughts and memory returned, she became filled with anguish to realise the iridescent flower was no longer safe with her. And then she became overcome with remorse, a remorse that she had been unable to prevent the theft. She found herself in her own cosy little bed, but gained no solace from this: she felt only the loneliness of her room and prayed her mother would not be far. With some difficulty, she sat herself up and looked out through her window. As ever, there stood her familiar view of trees. She contemplated them for a while and admired the beauty of their form.

Then: "Oh trees!" she cried out in anguish. "Why did you not stop them?"

She heard a noise in the living room adjacent as her mother hurriedly put aside whatever task was occupying her to rush to Floretta's side.

Floretta lay back again and sobbed. Her tears were bitter. They blinded her and she was glad her mother held her close so that she did not feel so completely alone in her grief.

"Oh mother," she wept. "Why didn't the trees stop them? Why didn't they help me? The forest blocked my way once, so why didn't it block their way? Why did the forest do nothing to protect its flower?"

"Hush. Hush now," murmured Flora. "When you are better, I will explain these things to you. But now you must rest. You must not disturb yourself with these unhappy thoughts. All will be resolved. Look, I am well. You have no need to worry on my account. Our sole problem is to restore you to health again. Stay still now and I will bring you some broth."

When Floretta had managed to eat a little, she felt slightly more cheered but still quite lost in her wretchedness. But no sooner had she lain back than she grew aware once more that, rather to her surprise, she had slept. It was now night. Her shutters were not closed – maybe her mother had feared the noise would wake her – and she could see the darkness outside. There was no moon and, in the complete blackness that was this night, no glimpse of the forest or of any tree. "Good," thought Floretta. "I do not want to see them. I have not forgiven them."

After some minutes, she noticed the figure of her mother sitting at her bedside, quiet and motionless in the still darkness. As Floretta stirred, so did her mother: she rose from her chair and threw aside the living room door: a rush of cooling air issued in from the unoccupied chamber, with it the weak candlelight the woman had sought. She approached her daughter, her kindly features now softly illumined.

"Floretta," she began, stroking the tousled locks gently aside from the tear-stained face. "There is something I must explain to you. Let me tell you first that I too, at times, felt even as you do now, before, that is, I reached a greater understanding; I too, wondered at the apparent impassivity of the forest, at its failure to act. But now I realise – and want you to understand too – that it is most unfair to blame the forest for evils perpetrated by human beings…

"The forest is timeless and ageless, this we know, but scarcely omnipotent. Without being able to transform human nature, any effort by the forest to moderate the activities of humankind would seem paltry indeed. The forest is powerless to intervene and, moreover, is debarred from doing so. Nature has assigned the forest a passive role – but nonetheless an important one – to exert a steadying influence over all life throughout the many ages of time – before and beyond the coming of the human race. As spectator of countless outrages, the forest has frequently longed to become more active, but throughout endless aeons has found no way to change its role. Nature simply has not equipped it for action: activity is the preserve of humankind…

"We know ourselves that the forest has on occasions dared to take some small action to protect its loved ones; we have witnessed too its wariness of venturing too far – that same wariness for which you reproach it now. But please realise, to intervene openly in human affairs would be to provoke a confrontation in which the forest could never win. It would be a simple matter for people to lay waste the forest by way of revenge; it is nigh impossible for the trees to stage such an offensive against human beings…

"So, Floretta, you must lay aside your bitterness and reconcile yourself to the scheme of Nature. Do you understand now, little one?"

Floretta blinked sleepily; the long lecture had proved tiring. "Yes," she murmured before drifting once more into a peaceful, healing sleep.

CHAPTER 14

After two days Floretta felt sufficiently recovered to rise from her bed. By some miracle she had broken no bones, but her limbs were nonetheless bruised and painful. She could use her hands only with some difficulty, and her knees were so swollen she could not walk without considerable discomfort. Her long skirts had fortunately protected her legs from worse injury. But she needed to convalesce, and so she sat in a little wicker chair at the front of the cottage and soaked in the summer sun, while Flora busied herself with the daily chores on her own, just as Floretta had done only the previous summer.

As Floretta relaxed in the little chair one day, dozing in the drowsy warmth, she became gradually aware, as if in a dream, of the sound of movement about her. At first, the sensation of activity became absorbed into her dreaming and did not disturb her, but then, when someone spoke, she felt herself jolted into wakefulness.

"She must be asleep," whispered the voice, "which means that for the moment she is harmless…"

"Then let's seize her as she is and be off…"

"No, you fools, leave her," hissed a third voice. "I have told you she must come with good will."

"Is that possible?" Floretta recognised the first voice again. "Surely she will turn on us when she awakes…"

"That is a chance we must take. I tell you we will wait until she stirs…"

Relieved by this remark, Floretta remained just as she was, head drooping forward, eyes tightly closed, and even continuing a heavy laboured breathing as of sleep. She struggled to marshal her drowsy thoughts. Who were they? What did they want? Did they wish her ill? And what would they do when they realised she was only feigning sleep?

The whispers around her continued:

"Perhaps she's already awake…"

"Nonsense! We would have seen her stir…"

"Then we should wake her…"

"No! We mustn't anger her. That's what went wrong before: she was so full of wrath she neutralised the power of her talisman. It's quite clearly useless without her, as we found to our cost. That's why we must gain her co-operation: only she can revive its power. If we annoy her, all is lost."

The others appeared to concur with this reasoning, for the whispering ceased. Floretta could hear merely the sound of their heavy breathing as they drew closer and scrutinised her. What were they thinking? Their minds were so near and yet their thoughts infinitely distant and unreadable. And did she perhaps recognise any of the voices?

"I still say we take her now." To Floretta the speakers sounded almost embarrassingly close; it seemed even as if she could feel the warm draught of their breath. "It might be hours before she awakes. And if we wait too long, the other one will appear."

"That might be all to the good. Why don't we take them both while we're here? We can manage two women…"

"Yes, but not two witches…"

"Be quiet, you fools! Or else you'll waken her before we're prepared!"

There followed another pause.

"Are you sure this is the one we want, Colonel?" one of the voices asked at length.

"Yes, this is definitely the one. We were told the young one. And we're not taking the other. She's of no value and there is no sense in burdening ourselves with two…"

"Are you going to wake her then, Colonel?"

"We'll give her a few moments more… And remember, I do all the talking…"

Unable to restrain her curiosity any longer and realising that she could not maintain her act forever to any effect, Floretta stirred a little as of someone waking, blinked her eyes and looked up.

"She's stirring."

Floretta looked up into three faces, all of which were staring into her face with large solicitous eyes. The three were horsemen, members of the King's Guard, none of whom she recognised however. They were grouped very close about her, one resting on one knee, another bending around her from the side, and the third leaning forward hands on knees to peer deeply into her face. They obviously considered her an object of extreme curiosity.

As a backcloth to this distorted trio, all of whom appeared to possess large heads and fleshy hands but small bodies and tiny feet, stood a fourth guardsman, this one looking quite uninterested and staring off into the forest, patiently holding the reins of the four quiet horses. And beside him stood a small silver carriage, daintily beautiful, with one white pony in front and on top a coachman dressed in fine livery. From such a carriage one would expect a fine princess to step, but Floretta saw that the carriage was empty. The scene possessed an unreal quality. Could she perhaps be dreaming still?

An instant later the scene became more convincing: the three guardsmen stepped back from her and in so doing assumed more normal dimensions. Floretta addressed them boldly: "You are friends of the villain Elavisado," she stated bluntly.

"Indeed we are not," replied the most senior of the three – a refined gentleman – in a measured tone. "You are right that certain of my men have been here before, and in his company, but believe me when I say that none amongst us are friends of his. Our association with him has been through chance not choice. If I may introduce myself, I am Colonel Llorens, first officer of the King's Guard." He drew proudly to attention and bowed dutifully as he pronounced the words.

"In fact, My Lady," he continued, "the villain Elavisado – as you so rightly call him – was loath to return here today following the last unfortunate incident. The task of guiding this party fell to me. I should imagine he is consumed with shame at the memory of his most ungentlemanly conduct towards you. I was quite appalled to hear of the incident. My Lady, may I offer a most humble apology on his behalf; and will you please accept my word that no such conduct would ever be forthcoming from a member of the King's Guard!" And he bowed again, this time more deeply, but not so much to Floretta, more, it seemed, as a sign of respect to the name of his regiment.

Floretta pondered a few moments before replying: she had to be courageous and speak plainly if there were to be any hope of retrieving the flower. "I will accept," she said coolly, "that the King's Guard does not entertain violence towards women, but the King's Guard, it seems, is not above theft."

The Colonel stiffened at this slight but retained his dignity. "Indeed, My Lady, that is not how I would have interpreted the last mission here, but, if it is as you say, then it is for me to apologise for that matter too."

Floretta sensed treachery. "Why all these meaningless apologies?" she exclaimed, springing to her feet. "What do you want of me? You have stolen my beautiful flower, what else can you desire?"

"My Lady," continued the Colonel. "It is not for me to explain the unseemly seizure of your property on that recent occasion, but merely to deliver an official apology for it and, in return for the inconvenience you have been caused, to deliver an invitation to the Royal Palace."

"An invitation?" Floretta grew increasingly suspicious. She disliked the wording of the 'invitation'. When their remarks had not been intended for her ears, the implication had been different. "But why?" she asked. "What reason should they have for inviting me? Whatever do they imagine I could do for them?"

"I am not empowered to produce reasons for the desires of the Royal Household, My Lady, merely to present notice of them. Suffice it that your presence would be greatly appreciated by His Majesty the King and that, as a sign of goodwill, a carriage has been sent to convey you with comfort."

"But supposing I do not wish to go," she parried. "I know nothing of royal manners and I am happy here."

"In that event, I fear we must press you, for your arrival is awaited with some considerable impatience."

"But what must I bring with me and what must I wear?"

"You need bring nothing, My Lady," he told her. "All your needs will be attended at the Palace and all the clothing you require will be at your disposal."

Floretta knew there was a trick of some kind behind this seemingly gracious 'invitation', but she also knew that if she did not willingly go with them, they would force her, and there would be no escape from them: at the moment, she could not even run properly; her sore legs would not carry her far. And if she delayed, soon her mother would arrive and try to protect her, and then they would hurt her mother as she herself had been hurt. But above all, she was prepared to accept the risks involved in accepting the invitation because it seemed her only hope of ever being reunited with the flower. Her mind made up, she took a few slow steps towards the carriage.

"You know, Floretta, the hens are missing you." She heard her mother's gentle laughing voice calling from the side of the house. "They're just not so ready to peck for me. They are complaining!" She turned and saw her mother appear from the back of the cottage where she had been feeding the hens, collecting the eggs and tending the vegetable garden, usually Floretta's little jobs. The two women looked at each other, Flora at first uncomprehending.

Floretta yearned to stay.

"Floretta!" cried her mother. "Stop! Don't go with them!"

As she rushed forward, one of the guardsmen moved to block her way. "Keep back," he told her. "The child is summoned to the Palace and is glad to come. It is none of your business."

"None of my business?" she cried. "You are only kidnapping my child!"

If I am going, I must go soon, thought Floretta, or there will be trouble. "Mother, I am going to see the flower," she called as she stepped into the little carriage. "I will bring it back to you. Everything will be all right. I will come to no harm!"

As she closed the little door, the carriage at once lurched forward. The promptness of departure alarmed her and she leaned instinctively out of the window as if reaching out her heart to her home. She imagined she heard the coachman say "That was easy" and felt a sudden rush of fear. Her world turned about her as the coachman swung his vehicle through a full circle to return it the way it had come and, as it turned, Floretta saw her cottage disappear from view. She dashed to the other window, desperate to see her mother once more before they were gone. She was to be granted one short glimpse and the memory of that last moment was to remain with her. For somehow in her young face, in her youthful body, Flora looked suddenly very old.

CHAPTER 15

The journey along the rough narrow path that led through this overgrown, unfrequented area of the forest was not comfortable, despite the luxurious upholstery of the carriage, and Floretta was glad when it was over, even though that meant they had left her beloved forest behind. She would have been happier to travel on foot – not that she was currently fit to walk – but the guardsmen insisted on such speed that walking was clearly out of the question.

It was a relief to arrive in Torquella, so that the carriage could jog along the cobbled streets to which it was more accustomed, the wheels rumbling more rhythmically now with the clatter of the pony's hooves as a pleasing counterpoint. There was an urgency in the motion of the carriage which aroused in Floretta a feeling of expectation, as if she were at the beginning of a wonderful adventure. Reason denied this possibility, however: her mission was a serious one and she could foresee no scope for frivolity.

The streets were bustling with activity, and groups of people turned and watched the royal carriage as it rolled by, hoping no doubt for a glimpse of the occupant and clearly curious as to the reason for such haste. The carriage lurched and climbed: up and over the old stone bridge they clattered, down and along, and onto a fine tree-lined boulevard, and then at last into the Palace square at the top of the empty market place. As they turned grandly in through the wide Palace gates, Floretta could not suppress a touch of excitement.

Then the carriage swerved to the side. Instead of being taken to the main portal, central to the long sweep of building and in line with the fine gateway through which they had just passed (and which had already closed behind them), she was deposited at a minor entrance – which was somehow disappointing.

There was no ceremony. Without a word, the guardsmen surrendered their charge to a group of housemaids who were waiting to welcome her and who ushered her quickly inside. They eyed her with caution and remained a little distant and Floretta returned their look of uncertainty. They were of a variety of ages but all handsome and strong and all equipped with a smart uniform of long navy silk frock and lace pinafore. Floretta became aware that they in turn were eyeing her dress.

"Dare we present her to His Highness in those common skirts? A housemaid would not address a royal personage in such lowly attire…"

"But it will take time to change her…"

"And we all know with what urgency she is awaited…"

Floretta's spirits were downcast; she had never felt the rudeness of her clothing before. Meanwhile, apparently growing accustomed to the prospect of this lost little figure, the maids abandoned their wariness and all found their tongues at once:

"We can at least brush her hair…"

"Nice little face – if we powdered it…"

"Good idea, but dare we…"

"D'you fancy she'll let us? She looks sweet enough but…"

"You never know, do you? They say all witches look sweet…"

"What I want to know is, does she speak?"

This last quip was followed by a round of girlish giggles. But tomfoolery was clearly not allowed: the older lady present moved in quickly with a stern "Of course she does!".

"Arja… do you think she really is a witch?" resumed one of the maids after a pause.

"Well, so they say," replied Arja, the older lady, kindly. "They say she is, but rumour has it her powers are all for good and none for evil, so maybe she isn't."

"Hope you're right, Arja."

"Let's at least brush and powder her before we present her to the Prince, then."

"The Prince?" asked Floretta. Where others might have found themselves annoyed by the housemaids' impudent gossip, Floretta felt herself cheered by their good nature and free humour so that she now spoke up without thinking. "The Prince?" she asked again. "I was told I would see the King."

"You see, she can talk!"

"She wants to see the King!"

"Thought perhaps she only spoke to cast spells!"

"Maybe that was one!" More girlish giggles.

"Be quiet, girls!" The senior woman, Arja, became stern again. "You will remember that this young lady is a guest in our household. Observe your place!"

They curtseyed obediently. "Begging your pardon, Miss," they said. "Meant no harm, Mistress Arja."

"Yes, my dear." Arja addressed Floretta now. "I think later you will see the King. But first we must present you to the Prince."

"Do you mean the Prince Elbert?" Floretta asked.

"Goodness no, my dear," Arja replied. "I doubt if you will come to meet him."

Floretta could only feel comforted by this information: she had no desire for a re-enactment of their last embarrassing encounter.

"Why do you think that you might?" asked Arja pleasantly. "Do you admire him? Do you find him handsome? Well, the prince you will meet is even more handsome. You are to be presented to our Crown Prince, His Royal Highness Julien." She sat Floretta at a little dressing table and began brushing her hair.

"Julien, darling of the housemaids!" laughed one of the younger women, taking up a large puff and patting it into a porcelain powder bowl.

"Hold your tongue," rebuked Arja. "I will not entertain rumour-mongering."

"'Rumour-mongering'! Oh Arja, you are funny." And all the girls laughed, Arja with them, and Floretta for one moment almost wished that she too were a member of this jolly group as a housemaid in this fine palace.

"Nearly ready," they told her.

"Is Elbert Prince Julien's brother?" asked Floretta.

"Indeed not," answered Arja. "Why, how little you know of the Royal Household, my dear. They are cousins, not brothers."

"And so we should hope," added one of the younger maids. "Seeing that Elbert has just married Julien's sister!" This last piece of news came as a surprise but nonetheless as an additional relief to Floretta.

"Perhaps we should warn you not to speak of Elbert to Julien," another told Floretta. "For goodness' sake don't suggest to him that they're brothers!"

"Imagine. Wouldn't he be furious?"

"There is little love between the two," explained Arja.

"Is he often furious?" asked Floretta.

"Julien? Yes, quite often."

"But he's easy to please too, if you understand what I mean," added one of the young maids.

"Do you know why Prince Julien wishes to see me?" asked Floretta.

A knock came on an inner door of the room.

"We have some idea, but then that is for him to say…"

One of the maids opened the door and a man's voice was heard from the corridor beyond it: "The small carriage was seen to cross the square. The Prince wishes to know whether the young lady has arrived safely and, if so, when she will be ready to be received into his presence. His Highness is at present awaiting her arrival in the Long Gallery and I am required to escort her there."

Floretta stood up, watching her shabby work dress rise with her in the mirror, but thankful for the neat hairstyle the maids had so quickly given her. "You'd better go," the maids whispered. "Good luck! It's all right, you look lovely!"

CHAPTER 16

Floretta had considered this first room grand enough, but now she stepped from what was in actual fact the housemaids' cloakroom into a corridor so broad, so high and so light as to dwarf it. She felt almost dizzy; walled with mirrors and spaced with tall pillars the corridor seemed to stretch forever in both directions. The gentleman set off to the right and Floretta obediently followed him, suddenly to realise they were not alone: two guardsmen had moved into position a few steps behind. The four kept pace, their footsteps echoing rhythmically back and forth along the strangely murmuring corridor.

As they proceeded along, Floretta gradually became aware of a group like themselves approaching from the other end: another butler was bringing a girl like herself to meet her, and they too had an escort of two guards. Just as she realised the man she could see was none other than her gentleman and the girl was in fact herself, they reached the glass wall that marked the corridor's end only to turn along another similar corridor to the side.

Looking behind, Floretta saw herself and her butler receding in yet another mirror, along with the two guardsmen who still maintained the same discreet distance, whereas the butler appeared to be gaining on her. He seemed almost to be running. Floretta wondered whether she should mention her sore knees but found she could not catch him to tell him. And she dared not call out in such an awesome reverend place.

They had reached a marble stairway, so fine and spacious an army could have ascended by it but so high that one had no idea where its gleaming balustrades might lead. To Floretta the glorious candelabra could well be hanging from heaven, and one could see only the tops of the tall archways which grouped themselves beyond the balustrades which marked the upper storeys. It seemed they were required to ascend, and so Floretta grimly applied herself to the task.

In pursuit of the butler, she reached the top of the main flight, only to find that the stairway continued with branches in three directions. They took the left one. At its top, more stairs came into view leading to higher floors but thankfully they remained on the first floor following more glass corridors. Suddenly the butler disappeared from the corridor to the side. Floretta stepped after him into a huge airy chamber. The pillars were so lofty that now, by comparison, the corridors afforded a memory of crampedness.

"This is the Long Gallery," the gentleman butler announced. "We are to wait here." He clapped his hands loudly, and within seconds, two servants appeared at the door, presumably from some position of circumspect concealment without. "Send word," he said. "Find the Prince. You must tell him, all is ready." With a bow they were gone, as quickly as they had come.

The Long Gallery had much to attract the eye. It was hung with large paintings, mainly portraits of royal persons in rich clothes, often on horseback, but now trapped for eternity in frames of precious metals. Alongside, thickly embroidered tapestries were hanging, mostly with abstract motif, and — towards the centre of the room — glass machines which whirred and tinkled and produced strange tricks of light and colour. The gallery was peopled with stone figures, sitting, standing, meditating. Floretta examined these for signs of life; it soon became clear the Prince was definitely not among them.

But the masterpieces of art claimed from Floretta no more than a cursory glance; far more interesting to her were the rows of pillars, thick and tall as tree trunks, and the high vaulting rising above the pillars, as intricate and graceful as the branches of the trees and surely modelled in their imitation. For a moment she felt almost at home. But then she found the pillars were smooth, completely smooth. What use were they like that? They lacked the carved bark patterns which adorn the trunks of genuine living trees; there was no crevice for any tiny life to gain a hold. And the vaulting, it was solid; there were no spaces for shafts of sun or gentle breezes. Floretta span around in alarm: there were no windows to the outside world, no views of the sky! Indeed, light and air seemed to be brought to this room by unnatural means. Perhaps that was the function of the whirring glass machines…

One of the servants returned. "The Prince has been seen strolling in the gardens," he panted. "My colleague is seeking him there."

The butler reflected. "Then let us away to the gardens," he decided. And so they set off once more along the corridor in the direction from which they had only just come. Accordingly, the two guardsmen fell into place behind.

As they were descending the stairway they were met by the second servant. "His Royal Highness," he gasped, "is taking the air in the Water Garden and sends word that the young lady is to await him in the Library."

"Aha, the Library!" remarked the butler with a certain glee. "Now," he told the two servants. "Return to the gardens and observe the Prince, and if he demonstrates any further change of inclination, convey word of it to us in the Library immediately!"

The two departed downwards forthwith and Floretta saw that it was for her to head upwards again. Fortunately the Library was by comparison not far. The butler escorted her in and closed the doors, the guardsmen dutifully adopting their positions outside. "You may sit," he told her, "although I stand. I see that you are not used to large houses."

"Indeed no, Sir," she agreed, gratefully selecting a large upholstered chair which was at hand. It was so soft it appeared at first to devour her but proved so firm that it supported her with a mere caress. The Library was a pleasant room, warmed by the soft browns of leather-bound volumes and enriched by thick velvet curtains of many greens which guarded the tall windows: colours close to Floretta's heart. This room was evidently at the back of the Palace; there were windows, looking out across opulent views of the royal parklands.

Floretta began to relax; she felt at ease in the company of this gentleman, even though he was standing so formally. Presumably, in his long experience as gentleman in service, he had acquired the art of discreet presence, omnipresence without intrusion. He gave the room an almost friendly atmosphere.

Floretta lost herself in her thoughts only to find herself expressing them out loud. "I wonder what His Highness the Prince is like," she heard herself say, and then remembered she was not alone. "Oh! I beg your pardon, Sir. I did not mean to be forward… but… may I ask what manner of man is the Prince…" She had not meant to ask.

"My child…" smiled the butler. "Indeed you may ask – you need not question your right to question – there is no problem there. The problem is a different one, and mine. How might I answer? That is the problem with which you present me and by it I am beaten. Our Prince… I confess he is a man to defy gainful delineation."

Floretta was puzzled by these words. "Sir," she asked. "What manner of man do you mean? What… does he defy?"

"Defy?" He laughed. "What does he defy? Why, he defies all good sense and moderation and yet is a slave to convention! Such a man is our Prince. He is princely beyond all princeliness but whimsical beyond all whimsicality."

Floretta could only feel rather bemused. "That does not describe him very… clearly," she faltered.

The butler shrugged. "How can I describe him?" he asked rhetorically. "How can one describe the wind? He is quick, dashing and unpredictable. What more can I say? He is certainly handsome. Some call him dynamic and say he is passionately devoted to his work, but others term this… obsession. Aggressive, demanding, capricious… There you are!"

Floretta blinked in amazement. "I'm sorry Sir," she said. "But I can imagine no such person. Your words convey little meaning to me…"

"Do they not? Ah well, child, then you are beaten and not I, and I have won, for such was my intention. I have answered the impossible question truthfully and painstakingly and yet with complete loyalty to my master. For if my words conveyed you good meaning, would I have selected them?"

"Sir," said Floretta. "You speak in riddles…"

"Yes," he said. "And when the Prince asks, 'How then speaks Ashvy Parva of me', they will say, 'In riddles your Highness', and he will be pleased…"

Minutes ticked by, or at least so the large library timepiece informed them.

"The Prince is unavoidably delayed," observed the butler.

"Is he often delayed?" asked Floretta.

"Often," he replied, glancing at her sideways with a suggestion of a smile. "But then through no fault, you must understand, more through a positive quality of character."

The doors surprised Floretta as they flew open, even though she was waiting for them to do so.

"Be upstanding for His Royal Highness, the Crown Prince Julien!"

The butler stiffened himself and prepared for a respectful bow. Floretta sat up in her chair, consumed by a sudden alarm.

"Stand!" hissed the butler.

In time, she found her feet.

CHAPTER 17

Following the example of the butler, Floretta lowered her gaze. Nevertheless, she could scarcely restrain herself from some peeping, though careful not to raise her head before seeing the butler do so. It was obvious which of the group that entered was the Prince: he strode in, the others followed meekly; and moreover he was a striking young man, remarkable not in physique – his being of medium height only and of rather ordinary colouring, brownish hair and pale complexion – but in possessing a presence that demanded notice, an insistence of manner, a bold self-awareness. All waited on his word, all awaited his permission or craved his instructions.

"Surely the young lady is tired after her journey," he said haughtily. "I think she should be seated. Parva, escort her to a comfortable chair."

The chair of Floretta's own choice was no distance from her; she had scarcely just risen from it. Nonetheless, with an elegant gesture, Parva positioned his arm beside Floretta for her to steady herself as she stepped back to sit down once more. As the only seated person, Floretta felt herself suddenly conspicuous; the Prince's retinue remained standing deferentially with averted gaze. And yet she felt as though all eyes were on her.

"The young lady is doubtless in need of some refreshment. Parva, I am surprised that you had not thought to offer some. See to it at once that a suitable repast is brought for the young lady! And now you may all leave us."

The Prince's courtiers obediently filed out, but the butler appeared reluctant to conform. "But Your Highness," he murmured. "Do you think it's wise?.."

"Be off with you, Parva! It is not for you to question my wisdom. I wish to speak to the young lady alone, as you well know. Eager though you are, no doubt, to eavesdrop, I will not oblige you. For that reason have I given you a duty to perform. Attend to it!" He turned towards Floretta and smiled. "I do not need your assistance in coping with this gentle maid."

Without protesting further, Parva bowed extravagantly several times and backed from the room, closing the doors behind himself. The Prince watched him go, and when he had gone, turned and fixed his gaze on the 'gentle maid' instead. He crossed the room and sank into a soft chair facing Floretta, whence to survey her.

"Why are you so ill?" he asked at length, his voice marked by curiosity rather than concern. "You must sit back and relax. I must say I had expected someone rather sounder than yourself. Rumours spoke of a girl in radiant health. Radiant beauty in potential form I see upon you, but your state is such that your beauty lies dormant. You look somehow crumpled and weary…"

"I suffered at the hands of your men," she explained, overcoming her natural reserve. "Or perhaps I should say, at their feet."

The Prince failed to cross-question her on this. "You bruise quickly…" he remarked, sounding surprised rather than sorry.

"Sir, perhaps you misunderstand," she told him. "I was not injured today. Indeed, I am now much recovered. I am speaking of my encounter with your men a few days ago."

"Well!" he said. "I must say I did not know that my father's men were wont to handle matters so roughly!" His surprise sounded quite genuine. "Now I see the reason for their initial failure. I trust you will allow me to apologise for any discomfort caused you in mine or my father's name. Such is not our policy, let me assure you. I suspect our men are overzealous. It is difficult to censure them for such a failing. But enough of that; tell me, do you know why you are here? What intelligence have you been given?"

"No, Your Highness," she replied. "I do not know why I am here." (For, although she knew why she personally had come, she did not know why he had summoned her, or if indeed it was he who had done so.) "No one has told me anything."

A knock came upon the door. "Yes, what is it?" called the Prince impatiently.

The door opened. It was Parva, the butler, again. He bowed courteously but still the Prince looked annoyed at the interruption.

"Refreshment for the young lady, Your Highness," explained Ashvy Parva.

"Oh yes, of course. Well, be quick with it then and be off," muttered the Prince.

Parva ushered in four pretty maidservants, each bearing a well-laden tray. These they placed on a low table which Parva quickly conjured up from across the room and positioned before Floretta. All was completed at great speed, and within seconds, Floretta and the Prince were left as before. Floretta did not feel hungry even though presented with such a fine spread of fruits and delicacies, but politely sampled a sweetmeat.

"Where were we?" asked the Prince. "Ah yes, you were telling me what you had learnt so far during your visit here…"

"Yes," responded Floretta. "I have learnt very much, though I have not been here long, for I have never been inside a palace before."

"Quite so," agreed the Prince. "But that is not the matter in question. You must learn for what purpose you are here, for it is a matter of great urgency. How might I begin?" he asked himself. "Tell me, whom did you expect to meet when you arrived here? We will begin there. Whom do you expect to see, tell me that."

"I thought I might see the King," she replied. "Or maybe even…"

"Yes," he interrupted. "Your intuition is correct: you are here to see my father, the King. But, you must understand, you cannot be taken to him immediately. First you must, as it were, be prepared. You see, the King is a very old and extremely sick man. Have you any experience of nursing aged people?"

"Oh yes!" said Floretta. "I nursed my old grandmother when she was ill."

"Good!" he answered eagerly. "Indeed very good. Then my father's condition will be no shock to you, as it might be to some. Realise as well that, when you see him, he will be in his bedchamber and not in an audience room where he would prefer to receive visitors."

"But of course," agreed Floretta. "If he is very ill, it would be wrong to disturb him."

"Exactly," continued the Prince. "Now, it seems to me that next I must explain to you precisely why you have been summoned here. I imagine you probably consider you already know, now that I have informed you of my father's illness, but, I must tell you, there is more to this affair than shows upon the surface!"

The Prince spoke quickly and earnestly: "Young woman, I trust you, though many might not; I can see honesty and a love of justice in your face. And so the decision comes to me to entrust into your confidence various secrets concerning Affairs of State. My reason for the revelations I am about to make is that I must impress on you the urgency of the matter we are about: the very security of the State is at stake in it. In your power lies the *status quo*; it is for you to act to maintain it, to prevent, as might well otherwise ensue, a state of bloody civil war!"

"Speak on quickly," breathed Floretta, disturbed by the Prince's words and anxious to learn of the situation, though still she could not imagine how it could possibly involve her.

"My father's illness and the constant threat of his death," continued the Prince, "have precipitated a dangerous political situation. For years now, there has been an underhand plot to supplant me as Crown Prince in favour of my cousin, the Prince Elbert, and if my father dies soon, I may find myself powerless against it. You see, I have almost no authority against the conspirators: they stand high in this land: none other than my uncle, the Duke of Ferrar, the 'Grand Duke' as he calls himself, gives them their lead!..

"He is, I confess, an evil man: the methods he employs are even more wicked than his designs: my father has reached his old age – of necessity – but his decline is deemed inadequate by my uncle who has sought to further it! With poisons and spells, my uncle has undermined my father's health. Thus far I have been powerless to prevent him. He has distracted my father, administered foul potions masquerading as medicines to rob him of his reason and then turned him against me with evil rumours! Now on his deathbed, my poor father has agreed to surrender his kingdom; he has agreed to pass the Throne to my uncle in my place as regent until, to use my uncle's loathsome beguiling words, I 'reach a greater maturity'!

"My father is completely misled. As I am sure you can see, once my uncle has the Throne, he will not relinquish it as easily as he now pretends, and in time the Royal Line will be handed to his son, my cousin, the weakling Elbert."

Floretta was deeply shocked by all this news. "Your Highness," she said. "You have my deepest sympathy in your difficulties. Your poor father… I had no suspicion that events had taken such a dreadful turn in the Royal Household. If the people but knew…"

"Exactly," he replied. "But the people must not know. It must never come to their ears. Turmoil would result and turmoil we must prevent. It is the function of the monarchy to provide a certain stability, not to trouble the people with problems of State. I trust I have your confidence in this?"

"Most certainly, Your Highness," she assured him.

"Good," he nodded. "I knew when I saw you that I could count on your support. I recognised you truly as a loyal subject. We must apply ourselves quickly. Until now I have been on my own: since the death of my mother, there have been in this household only certain servants to bear my trust, and then I would not dare count on them. All responsibility has been mine and, unaided, all my efforts have been in vain. I have fought to maintain my father's life and health and have sought to mend my reputation in his eyes but so far to no avail. Time was always against me; the doctors insisted my father had only days, maybe even only hours, to live. The problem was always, how could I bring truth once more to his aged poisoned mind before it was too late… But now I have a powerful ally…"

"Oh, Your Highness," exclaimed Floretta. "If only I could help you too…"

"But my dear," replied the Prince. "As I understand it, you can help me. That is why you are here."

Floretta looked at him with large eyes, surprised and uncomprehending. He in turn regarded her with alarm.

"Why!" he insisted. "Are you so loath to admit it? Or are you not the maiden who possesses the Secret of Eternal Youth?"

CHAPTER 18

Floretta found herself unable to phrase any answer to the Prince's question. A more prudent young woman would no doubt have sensed danger immediately and quickly set about fabricating some story to extricate herself from the situation, but not only did Floretta lack the guile for fabrication, it did not occur to her. She was silenced not so much by a shortage of lies, more by a shortage of the truth. She could furnish no completely truthful answer; to reply 'yes' or 'no' would both be equally incorrect: she had never considered herself to be the guardian of any special secret, certainly of no secret which she could bequeath at will, and yet she was undoubtedly the maiden to whom the Prince was referring.

'The Secret of Eternal Youth' the Prince had said. These were the selfsame words used by the trickster Elavisado; it was none other than he who had coined the phrase. Floretta understood now the chain of events which must have preceded her 'invitation' to the Palace – events which someone more worldly would no doubt have suspected rather earlier, but which Floretta in her simplicity and artlessness had failed to realise until now.

She could see now that the rumours surrounding her grandmother's rejuvenation and the wonderful health of them both had spread even to the Royal Household, undoubtedly by the activity of Elavisado's tongue. Moreover, the responsibility incumbent on her to restore the King to health was now very apparent. What an important figure she had suddenly become in the World of Man!

But no great feeling of power pulsed through her at this thought; rather, a sensation of sadness and an inkling of despair. That she could fulfil the task before her seemed no more than a very remote possibility. For it was the flower that had renewed her grandmother's youth and not she, even though, as she understood it, she had herself been somehow involved. Certainly without the flower to help her, there could be no hope, and she now began to doubt whether she would ever be reunited with it. She could see, therefore, no way of ever regaining possession of the flower, no way of returning it to its place with her mother, no resumption of their happy life together. Her own small hopes were shattered. Her future now depended on the whim of this Prince.

And so, as Floretta's thoughts returned eventually to the Prince, the silence began to hang heavy on her; she feared the Prince's reaction, wondered as to his thoughts as he eyed her so suspiciously, so strangely, and wished that he would express them. What were his intentions for her now? They could not be good – he could be feeling only frustration and anger towards her – but she wished to wait no longer before knowing.

"I still hear no reply to my question," she heard him say at last. "It could be that you have now forgotten it, in which case I am prepared to repeat it, for I must know the truth. Or it may be that you have simply chosen to ignore it, in which circumstance I will not repeat it as I refuse to be pressured by insolence. It could be, however, that you failed to understand it (or at least that you decide to pretend so) so that I am required to rephrase my question more simply."

"There is no need, Sir," replied Floretta meekly. "I beg your pardon for not replying to your question, as I both remember and understand it… It is merely that I do not understand how I should answer…"

This was clearly seen as a further annoying evasion. Floretta watched the Prince attempt to control his annoyance and heard him reply quietly, "But you must surely know whether you are the girl I have been seeking to assist in saving my father's life."

"Yes, I believe I am that girl."

"There has been no mistake? You are quite convinced?"

"I believe not…"

"And you understand what you say?"

"Yes, My Lord…"

"Then you are the keeper of the secret I desire! What more is there to say? What must I do so that you will feel free to admit it? Have I treated you so badly? I wish you no ill; you will suffer no persecution for your powers."

"But I fear I have no powers, I have no secret…" pleaded Floretta.

"Then you contradict yourself. You cannot be the girl I sent for. She has been abducted and you have stolen her identity! You are an impostor and an ill-prepared one at that! This conspiracy will be unearthed with good speed for I see that my enemies have sent you to perplex and delay me! Confess soon, I advise you, and tell me this minute who brought you here!"

"It was the King's Guard, I believe…" she stammered.

"You believe? What do you mean, you believe? Either you know or you do not know. What was the name of the officer in charge of the mission?"

"Err… Colonel… Llorens, I believe…"

"How many men accompanied him?"

"Three. No, four. No! Five, counting the coachman!" she gasped, confused by this sudden barrage of questions.

"You don't really know, do you?" he accused. "You answer correctly but you do not remove yourself from suspicion. I can see that you have merely been versed with appropriate replies!"

He seized a silver handbell from the library table and rang the delicate thing viciously. With scarcely an instant's delay, the doors opened and Ashvy Parva sedately entered. Parva bowed very low: "You have a wish, Your Highness? It is my command…"

"Yes!" the Prince declared. "See to it that Llorens, first officer of the King's Guard, is summoned to my presence here with every possible haste, and immediately thereafter two of the most trusted men from my own personal guard!"

"With every possible haste, Your Highness," agreed Parva, bowing once more as he made his exit.

"And fetch that scoundrel Elavisado!" called the Prince as an afterthought.

"The scoundrel Elavisado, Your Highness," echoed Parva as the doors closed.

Then the Prince turned his wrath upon Floretta once more. "Shortly," he began, "I shall check with the Colonel whether you are the same girl he brought, and then I shall begin to know the truth. Either my enemies substituted you before the good Colonel in all good faith collected you, or else the mission was intercepted later after he had delivered you!

"If the latter, then I have uncovered treason in my own household… If the former, then the affair promises to be of less significance, restricted to one miserable villain and his foolish accomplice! Which is it? On your life tell me that! Are you in league with that trickster Elavisado? Is his whole story fiction? If so, we shall find him and he will hang. And you, what shall I do with you? I can assure you that you are beyond hope of escape or rescue now, however much your smooth-talking partner may have persuaded you otherwise… Your fate lies in my hands now, and your life depends on your co-operation with me!"

Floretta was so terrified she could not speak. She could merely shake her head in an effort to deny the accusations. Unfortunately this sign became misinterpreted.

"Ah! So you refuse to co-operate with me!" exclaimed the Prince. "To what gain I cannot imagine. I have sent for the most loyal of my own personal guard. If necessary, they will assist me in extracting the truth from you. But I hope that the unpleasant methods such as my men are keen to employ will prove unnecessary. I prefer a solution by more amicable means." He paused and took a deep breath. "You need only speak the truth to all my questions." His manner was now almost polite again. "First, I ask you girl, what do you see in me? What am I?"

"You, you are a prince, Sir," she stammered. How else could she reply?

"Just so!" he agreed. "And now I will tell you what I thought to see in you: an honest peasant girl who respected the Supremacy of the Throne. Was that first impression incorrect? Honest you are showing yourself not to be, it seems, but respect, respect you should possess nonetheless. How speak you on this?"

"Indeed, Sir," she replied. "I have always respected the Throne."

"Good. Then respect me now," he told her, "as first in succession in this land. And admit your deceit. I suspect that my original judgement of you was correct; you are merely a simple peasant maid, as honest as most, involved in this ugly affair through no malice, no treasonous intent. And therefore I am prepared to grant you a complete pardon for the unwitting part you have played."

Floretta was amazed at this apparent change of heart, this volte-face; she could not understand it.

"And moreover," continued the Prince, "to ensure your complete co-operation with me, I offer you many times the sum you have been tempted with. Name it and I will quintuple it! All I ask is that you give me details of the plot, how the trick was arranged, exactly who was responsible – name everyone involved – tell me where and when it took place, and why, if you know… Tell me these things, my dear, and you will receive only kindness from me and know no punishment from my hand. For I am just."

The Prince paused on this note of self-praise, but before Floretta could begin to reply, they were interrupted by a loud knock upon the door.

"Why so peremptory, Parva?" demanded the Prince as his butler entered.

"Your Highness." Parva bowed. "I pray you will excuse the eagerness of my manner but my task, at your request, is to be completed with every possible haste. I wish to announce the arrival of Colonel Llorens, first officer of the King's Guard!"

"Ah, so he is here at last," answered the Prince. "My compliments to your zeal, my good man, on this occasion you have done well. Allow the Colonel to enter. I trust you have also obtained the personal guardsmen I requested?"

"But of course, Your Highness. They wait here upon your command."

"Then entreat them to enter immediately on my given signal. You yourself, Parva, hasten meanwhile to my father's apartments and bring me word of any development in his condition."

"Your Highness, I hasten and I bring word." Parva bowed and returned to the door. "Colonel Llorens!" he called. "His Royal Highness awaits your presence!"

CHAPTER 19

With immaculate uniform and impeccable bearing, the Colonel marched smartly in and saluted his prince. He spoke no word and remained respectfully at attention.

"We have here," the Prince told Floretta with a certain pride, "a most loyal and trusted servant of the realm. One word from him will expose you certainly for what you are." Now he addressed Llorens: "Colonel," he began, "I have only one question to put to you, and it concerns this young woman. Is this the same girl whom you were sent to collect today and whom you delivered here? Or is she some other?"

"Your Highness," replied Colonel Llorens. "There is no doubt. I can swear that this is none other than the girl I brought today on your instruction."

"Thank you, Colonel," answered the Prince. "Your words console me. I can reveal now that there has been a plot to substitute an impostor, but I can at least rule out subversion in my own household. This girl was a fraud before you collected her! In league with the swindler Elavisado she sought to deceive me for personal gain, and now she ignores all my entreaties to confess! For the good of the State she will be seized and thrown into confinement!"

"Your Highness…" The Colonel seemed to hesitate before speaking. "Your Highness, if you will forgive my forwardness in speaking out, I would inform you of the confusion I perceive here. As I see it, the young lady cannot in any way be allied with Elavisado. His treachery I doubt not, but had the young lady been involved in it, would she have allowed herself to suffer as she did at his hands? Could any villain so abuse a partner and hope to retain that partner's trust? Why, she still bears the marks of his assault upon her."

"Colonel, I understand you not," declared the Prince, quite ignoring the point made. "I have established beyond doubt that this girl is not the sorceress I have been expecting. I have been thoroughly tricked by this girl and now you attempt to protect her! What interest have you in her? Has she beguiled you? My good man, are you somehow involved in this affair? How it grieves me to imagine that a trusted officer could have stooped so low! Is our Colonel the vehicle by which the conspirators hope to secure the release of their accomplice here? Llorens, is it you who were selected to introduce her in the first place?"

Sinking on one knee, the Colonel almost prostrated himself before the Prince. "Your Highness!" he besought the Prince. "You know me for your humblest servant! Distrust me not! Do not repay my earnest concern for you in this way! I seek merely to assist you. If the girl is guilty as you say, then I have no desire to shield her or to impede justice…"

"Colonel," replied the Prince sadly. "I long to believe you, for I know you have served my father long and well. But his life is at stake in this matter. I can take no chances." He rang his silver bell once more and two young officers entered sharply, eager as if ready for action and hoping for a skirmish. Their uniform differed from that of the King's Guard: they wore a more striking flamboyant red. "Take this man into custody," the Prince ordered them. As he said it, his voice wavered. "And hold him secure until you receive my word. Allow no one access to him, but see also that no harm befalls him."

They seized Llorens, who made no further protests, and the group was soon gone from the room. But before the doors could be closed, Parva the butler had slipped in.

"What news?" inquired the Prince distractedly.

"Your Highness," Parva informed him. "The condition of your father the King is at present unchanged; there has been no further relapse, but the doctors continually fear for him nonetheless: thus spake Karezza Avicenna, the chief physician."

"The news is reassuring," answered the Prince, "though not good. And the scoundrel Elavisado," he asked. "You have him waiting, I trust?"

"Alas, Your Highness," replied Parva. "Here I must admit defeat. Many are searching for him: at his residence, on the market place, in the taverns. As yet, none has reported any success. Rumour has it among his acquaintances, it appears, that he has taken to hiding through fear of reprisal from a witch he has wronged…"

"A witch?" exclaimed the Prince. "He has no witch. No doubt he refers to this child here! It is part of his trick. More like he fears reprisal from a prince!" He examined his butler more closely. "But your inefficiency is quite exceptional, Parva," he remarked, "and disturbing to say the least. Do I perceive that you too are involved in this plot to hinder me in my affairs? I need not ponder long to decide in whose pay you would therefore be…"

"Your Highness knows better," replied Parva drily. "I am deeply offended."

"That may well be," conceded the Prince guardedly. "For your sake and mine I hope my trust is well placed. But you remain warned. You are aware of the punishment that would befall you. You may leave my presence now, but remember: do not fail to communicate to me any relevant news you may collect."

CHAPTER 20

During these interruptions, Floretta had had some time to collect her thoughts so that, when the Prince turned his attention to her once more, she felt better prepared to answer him.

"Now, young woman," he said. "I have been very frank with you. You know my mind. You know the penalties which threaten you. And so, I must know your mind. Speak now!"

And Floretta knew that she must, though the task of explaining her position and bringing truth to the Prince appeared formidable. "You asked me, Sir," she began quietly, "to name all those with whom I have been involved… You suggest that I am an accomplice of the villain Elavisado… I must aver most strongly that I am not. He is known to me, of course, but is not in the least liked by me. I admit that he has before now approached me at my home, in search of spells for perfect health – as he would put it, not I – but as my trust for him is scant, I have desired no association with him. It was by no arrangement with him that I came here. I am not his accomplice, and he is not mine; in fact, I have no accomplice, for I have no business. I came here, as you are correctly informed, in response to an invitation, politely delivered by your good Colonel Llorens…"

Floretta's gentle voice seemed to exert a soothing influence on the Prince: never loud and demanding, nor shrill and insistent, instead mild and whispering, it came like a kiss upon the ear, a soft breeze, a rustling of leaves… All trace of the Prince's former emotion disappeared: he appeared to study her words attentively, dispassionately.

"How then can you say that you are not the girl I have been expecting?" he asked quietly at length.

"But Your Highness," she replied. "Forgive me, but never have I said that I was not. I have merely attempted to explain that there is some misunderstanding about my abilities…"

"Is that so?" he mused. "Well, if you are the girl concerned, I can scarcely believe you are not possessed of some valuable magical power. The rumours all indicate otherwise and they cannot be entirely without foundation of truth, I feel sure… And, I realise, even now you have thrown a spell over me – I sit here momentarily benumbed!" It seemed, however, that the spell – lightly and fortuitously cast – had as easily been broken: the Prince's newly found equability was evaporating visibly: his expression quickly resumed its characteristic intensity. Yet placidity was not replaced by anger: he seemed instead somehow pleased with Floretta. "Your reluctance to admit your abilities," he declared with satisfaction, "is none other than the traditional reluctance of weavers of spells!"

Floretta shook her head sadly.

"You are doubtless aware," he continued, "that for fear of weakening their powers, the foremost practitioners refuse even to speak of them! And stronger still is the fear of inciting the wrath of ill-wishers and other potential opponents. However, you need fear no wrath or opposition from me, if you are prepared to help me. If, nonetheless, you still wish to remain silent, then I ask you to give me a sign, that I may be really sure of you."

"Alas, Sir," she pleaded. "I doubt not your good intentions and would freely admit my power if, that is, I had possession of any. But I have none and can give you no sign. What do you wish me to do? I cannot cause chairs to rise towards the ceiling, nor birds to appear from the sleeve of my robe, nor the sky to grow dark and flash with lightning. Likewise, sadly, I cannot bring youth to an aged king…"

"How then," he asked, "do you explain the rumours surrounding your person? There must be an element of truth. Or are you ignorant of them?"

"No, Sir," she replied. "I am acquainted with these rumours."

"Are they then unfounded?" he pressed. "What of the story that you are responsible for the amazing youthfulness of your own mother, so that she appears senior to you only in maturity and wisdom? Do you discount this tale?"

"Sir," she told him haltingly, wary of compromising her dear mother. "What you say of my mother is true. But though I am aware of my mother's beauty, and though it pleases me, I cannot claim to have caused it. But then, neither by herself did she… I will gladly act as a nurse to your father," she went on. "I will do my utmost to cure him, but I cannot promise to be of any greater assistance than the nurses and physicians already in attendance…"

"The rumour," he continued, making no comment on her offer, "concerned a remarkable flower which was said to be responsible. What say you of that?"

"It is true," she replied, her heart beating faster, "that my mother and I possessed a special flower from the forest, which was stolen from us recently. Indeed, I do suspect it had more power than I…"

"Ah! Then you admit that the flower is your amulet for health and youth?"

"Our amulet? Oh Sir, now you confuse me once more, for I know nothing of amulets and can conceive no simple answer…"

The Prince did not pursue his point; as before he seemed more interested in his questions than in her replies. "I was originally convinced as to the magic of this flower," he told her. "Its appearance is so spectacular. But my confidence in it has since waned. It shows no great propensity for health, least of all of its own. It appears useless. I suspect its magic requires some skilled manipulation…"

"Then you have the flower?" breathed Floretta.

"Most certainly I have," he admitted.

"Then take me to it," she implored. "I long to see it. It will need my attention."

"Gladly," he agreed. "It rests at present in my father's bedchamber. We will go there forthwith."

CHAPTER 21

Along more and still more of the Palace's spacious echoing corridors, Floretta accompanied the Prince. Now that she was to be reunited with her beloved flower, an eagerness infected her stride and she forgot the pain in her limbs. Mirrors, marble, portraits, pillars, she was becoming used to them now. And the frankness of Prince Julien with her, plus the informality of their interview, had encouraged her no longer to feel so overawed by the Palace or by his presence.

The Prince was capable of great anger, to be sure, an anger to which she in her simple daily life had been quite unaccustomed. But he seemed to curb his anger so quickly, to be able so readily to change his mind and adopt a different attitude, that she did not really fear him. With all probability, he would soon release Colonel Llorens, and with equal probability, apologise to his butler for the insults directed at him. Floretta was now feeling rather more hopeful that the Prince would not prevent her from leaving the Palace when the time came, and that he would allow her to take the flower.

They passed many doors, ignoring each one, and paused at length before a portal of especially grand dimension and decoration, its door fashioned and polished from some exotic wood of unusual solidity and richness. Upon the door, there was a fine royal crest, and, at each side, there stood no fewer than four men-at-arms, at ease but smartly so. In acknowledgement of the arrival of their Prince, all shifted sharply to attention, moving with a precise and alarming simultaneity as if guided by some silent command. They offered the Prince and his guest no hindrance, so that the pair passed at once through the doorway and entered what Floretta presumed to be the King's apartments.

The room in which they first found themselves was by all indications a private sitting room. Its furnishings were of an exquisite beauty and perfect taste, which added to the general impression of elegance, comfort and light. A welcoming fire burned in the open hearth; a large dog lay stretched out on a deep-pile rug before it. As the two entered, the creature's eyes flickered momentarily in their direction but it did not stir to greet them.

"My father's dog Bruno," explained the Prince. "He pines. I fear he will die with my father."

He paid the animal no attention and, without pausing, headed straight across the room towards another door. Even here, the Prince did not knock or wait but opened the door immediately and entered, ushering Floretta in with him. The room was in darkness, a darkness so complete after the brightness of the other chamber that, once the Prince had closed the door behind her, Floretta found herself blind: lost and bewildered in a sea of blackness.

As vision gradually returned, she perceived that there was however some light: though the room contained no means of illumination whatsoever, the strong sunlight without struggled to discover a way in and located the merest of chinks between the heavy drapes. Floretta became aware that there was a bed in the room, then that there were other people. The bed itself was occupied by a languid figure that offered no response to their arrival, and grouped about it were others who assumed postures of agitation.

"Your Highness!" softly chided an elderly but sprightly gentleman in a long white robe, wagging a decorous finger at the Prince. "Remember your father's condition! You should not enter at such haste! And, unannounced!"

"Good Avicenna," replied the Prince. "None remembers my father's condition more than I. I bid you now, pick no quarrel with me in his presence – our differences will be settled at some more opportune moment, I assure you. For the moment, you and your colleagues may withdraw."

"But Your Highness," complained the physician. "If His Majesty should..."

"Master Avicenna!" insisted the Prince. "If we wish to avail ourselves of your services, we will soon recall you, have no doubt of that. But, for now, be gone!"

"Very well, My Lord," he conceded. "We will retire and await your command in the physicians' antechamber."

"So be it," replied the Prince.

As soon as they were gone, the Prince turned to Floretta who, in her uneasiness, had not moved from her position near the door.

"Approach the bedside," he requested. "And look upon our patient more closely. What think you?"

Floretta leaned cautiously over the bed and through the gloom discerned the crumpled form of the dying King. "He is so still," she whispered. "Are you sure that he still lives?" She could see no hope of life continuing in such a shrivelled body.

A weak voice issued from the slack lips: "If death is lassitude, then I no longer live, so that you will not hear my words as I speak them now and will not reply. But if death is new life and vigour, then I regret it is still eluding me…"

Prince Julien gripped his father's thin hand and gently kissed it. "Oh, My Lord," he breathed. "How deep is my happiness that I hear you speak to me once more! And how great is my joy that your condition is therefore improved! My faith that I will soon see you restored to health is further strengthened…"

Floretta could hear that the Prince almost wept.

"But, my son," murmured the weak voice. "I am an old man. Life holds nothing for me; I can no longer rule my kingdom. I have no wish to be restored to health. I desire only to rest… That you intend well, I doubt not, but do not hold me back from my resting place…"

"My father," choked the Prince. "You must not speak this way!"

And then Floretta saw that he did weep.

Floretta felt moved to emotion with the Prince, but was withheld from tears by embarrassment, by the feeling that she should not be present at this intimate interview. She wished to excuse herself – she could scarcely leave such august presence without doing so – and yet to do so would be to intrude her own self further. She could only stand as still as possible.

At length the Prince regained a state of greater calm. He tucked his father's limp hand once more under the bedcovers and turned back to Floretta. "I think my father is sleeping again," he whispered.

"I most certainly am not," responded the old King in a stronger voice. He had now even opened his eyes. "What now, my son," remarked the King. "Still womanising I see." His eyes were on Floretta. "Did your new mistress wish to sample the sovereign presence before time denied her the chance?"

"Alas Father, no," insisted the Prince. "As ever you misunderstand. This is no mistress of mine, else would I dress her in peasant's garb? No, Father, she is a nurse, a talented young nurse whose reputation grows daily. She has a gift with living things, a delicate touch… I am sure she can help you and ease your pain… Why, she is the maiden who reared the wonderful flower I brought you!"

"Oh, my son, my son," sighed the King, the energy in his voice rapidly fading. "As ever you talk too much and tire me. If your nurse can ease my pain then allow her; thus would you truly assist me. But leave me in peace now. Talk no more. I must sleep…" His breathing became heavy.

"He sleeps now," whispered the Prince.

"Perhaps he only feigns sleep," suggested Floretta.

"I think not," he said. "Of late, he is easily weary. Sometimes, he appears to improve, but it is always short-lived. If only we could sustain the improvement. What think you? Can you help him?"

"I have sworn already that I will do my utmost to cure him," replied Floretta, "but, as you fear, it may not be possible. I suspect he is in much pain, for he speaks of death and appears to have lost the will to live. It is for us to restore that will to him. I know not how; but in my heart I wish him and the kingdom well, and it may be that there is a power in my wishing."

"Let us hope that," he replied. "I will return your flower to you that it may assist you. But first, I must forewarn you as to its condition."

"Its condition?" Floretta could not conceal a note of alarm from her voice.

"Yes," he explained. "I fear we have not been as successful as you in tending it…"

"But did you not water it?" she asked.

"Oh yes," he said. "When I took delivery of it, I saw at once that it drooped and so with no delay it was watered…"

"What then, did it not improve?"

"Scarcely… And so I sent for the Royal Gardener…"

"And what did he do?" she demanded.

"Well, we assured him that it had been watered, but nonetheless he watered it again…"

"It does not like too much water," she complained bluntly.

"Alas, we did not know that," he told her. "We attempted our best. We could not identify the species, though the greatest of experts were consulted. At length they declared it to be a 'Forest Asphodel' and made their recommendations, and the Royal Gardener brought rich soil, compost, humus, moss…"

"It thrives in the forest soil!" she blurted.

"Shhh!" He cast a glance at his father but the old man had not stirred. "How could we know?" he asked. "We tried everything else. But whatever we tried, it continued to wither…"

"To wither? You mean it has already withered? You have allowed my flower to wither?" Never had Floretta known such anger in herself; she felt dizzy with the incomprehension of it. And the need to restrict her voice to hushed whispers served merely to intensity her frustration rather than to quieten it. She was urged to raise her voice to the Prince: if the flower was dead, she no longer feared annoying him; all was lost to her; to inform him of his stupidity and bad management would be an apt expression of her grief. She was restrained from doing so in an appropriate tone of voice not at all by fear but solely by her consideration for the ailing King. "Why did you not send it back to me," she hissed, "when you saw that you could not tend it? Or else, send for me earlier! Where is it now? I must see it at once."

"But it is here," he assured her, attempting to placate her. "In this room, as I have told you. I will fetch it for you." He started across the room.

"How can it be?" she accused. "If it were here, I would see it. Its brilliance, its glow, it shines through all darkness."

"Its glow is gone," he told her. "As it withered, so did its many hues fade and likewise its brightness. But now that you are here, you will be able to revive its colour and make it flourish again." He handed Floretta a pot which, in the obscurity of the darkened room, appeared to contain a shrivelled weed.

Floretta looked at it. "It is almost completely dead," she announced, her anger now moderated by a feeling of helplessness, a resignation to her grief. "As you have long known. And for its death, you must bear responsibility, not I. I fear you have made a tragic mistake in this, for without this flower, I can see no hope for you or me, no hope for your family or mine."

But he would not accept this. "There is still time," he insisted, and it was he who shouted: "There must be!" Then he attempted to moderate his voice as he remembered his father. "The flower still lives," he whispered, "and so does my father. So there is hope. Whatever mistakes have been made, they can still be righted. You need only act quickly!"

A prince who expected miracles from a common maid! Floretta did not trouble to argue with him further but rushed instinctively towards the window and began tugging at one of the heavy curtains.

"What are you doing?" he demanded. "My father prefers a darkened room!"

"You tell me to act, then complain when I do so," she answered. "What do you want me to do? I am taking my flower to the light of the day. Do you not know, does your gardener not know, that flowers need daylight? All green things need daylight." She placed the pot on the sill.

"No!" he called. "You will waken my father and he will not be pleased!"

"But why will he not be pleased?" she reasoned. "Does he not know that all living things, not just the flowers, need daylight? Do the physicians not know this? Daylight is good for people. So, for what reason must this room be darkened? Who has misled your father into believing it is good for him?"

The Prince was beginning to listen.

"And there is no air," continued Floretta. "Your father needs fresh air. He needs to go out into the forest. All is healthy in the forest where the air is pure, where the breezes are clean and scented with pine needles and dew. Nothing can live locked in an airless evil-smelling night."

"I think perhaps you are right," he told her. "There is much truth in your words. We have been continually misled in this household, I fear, by charlatans and fools, and by corrupt physicians who are the hirelings of my enemies. I trust not their meddlings and potions. We will try your remedies."

Together they began dragging aside the heavy velvet draperies so that a shaft of bright sun now fell directly onto the King's bed. Floretta flung open a casement so that a cool breeze blew on her cheek, bringing a transient memory of her home, and then rushed in past her to mingle with the unhealthy fug of the bedchamber.

"See, he is stirring again," whispered Floretta. And indeed, so the old King was; he appeared to be attempting to push himself upwards, as if to see out through the window. His son rushed to his side to assist him.

At that moment in came Karezza Avicenna, the chief physician. "What is going on?" he exclaimed. "I suspected something would be amiss by now! Your Royal Highness, respect for your rank I have indeed, but as I am responsible for your father's life, I feel I must complain most strongly at this interference! His Majesty does not want daylight in this chamber; he is not ready for exposure to sunlight. And furthermore, he is prone to draughts, so close that window, girl!"

"Leave the window as it is," the Prince ordered Floretta, seeing that she was about to obey.

"And medical considerations aside," continued Avicenna, "His Majesty has specifically requested a darkened bedchamber. He feels that he can rest better and that death, when it comes, will advance more easily and peacefully."

"A baseless notion!" declared the Prince. "Would that I knew who had planted such a chimera in my father's head! Someone is responsible for turning his mind!"

"I see you are prepared to deny your father his last wish," commented Avicenna, evading the implied accusation. "Nevertheless, I must insist that the windows and curtains be closed immediately for medical reasons!"

The King was now sitting up, gazing with an expression of contentment towards the window, himself expressing no complaint about his new treatment. Floretta watched him closely for any danger sign, the Prince and the physician both apparently ignoring him, and listened in to their duel of words, hovering between closing the curtains and opening them further as first one, then the other appeared to gain the upper hand in the argument.

The King looked stronger already, Floretta imagined: he seemed wide awake and appeared as if fascinated by the bright sunbeam which reached down and greeted him through the gap in the curtains. He blinked with surprise at the unexpected emanation. And gradually his wrinkled sallow old face began to relax and his features took on an expression of great joy, as if reflecting some inner illumination, an inner sense of relief, of ease, an inner conviction of greater knowledge gained, of experiencing the ultimate revelation. He cried out jubilantly, "It's time! I will go now!"

Deeply alarmed, the physician and the Prince aborted their argument and rushed forward to the King, attempting to calm him and make him lie back.

"My apprentice!" cried Avicenna. "I need my apprentice! Summon my apprentice Gerard from the antechamber!"

Floretta herself moved to do this but was not needed, for in response to this cry of urgency the said apprentice had appeared forthwith. "Master!" he called. "I attend!"

"A sedative!" replied Avicenna. "Quickly, quickly, a sedative! You will find it already mixed."

Fearful that something was indeed seriously wrong, Floretta began closing the curtains once more, leaving the pot with the pathetic remains of her flower behind them in the sunlight on the window sill. The King meanwhile insisted on pulling himself free from Avicenna's grasp and moving forward into the pool of light on his bed.

"It is time!" he cried as the curtains closed, gazing in wonder towards the window and raising a hand into the remaining shaft of light. "I must go now!"

Floretta now succeeded in pulling the heavy curtains tightly together, but still the King was undeterred; it seemed the light was still visible to him. He would not lie back, despite the combined efforts of the physician and the Prince. The apprentice returned bearing a tumbler and accompanied by two of the other physicians who hastily relieved Avicenna of his task of restraining the King so that he could attempt to administer the drug. Predictably, the King would not drink.

"The needle, Gerard! It must be the needle!" called Avicenna.

The apprentice made haste.

The bed was wide, and the King difficult to reach and to hold. He pushed them all away with ease, for they were fearful of grasping his frail limbs too tightly. "Enough, Sirrah!" he told Avicenna, sweeping the tumbler from his hand so that it shattered across the floor. "Don't hold me back now!"

The King moved across his bed away from them all and rose up. But then his sudden strength was arrested by an ugly choking noise from his throat. He held his body suddenly rigid but only for a few moments before collapsing heavily, his kingly grace now gone, upon the rich carpet of his floor. At that moment there began a scratching noise at the door, and a pitiful whimpering, as from some poor creature injured and trapped.

CHAPTER 22

The apprentice Gerard and the two assistants hurriedly ministered to the fallen body of the King. "Your Highness…" Karezza Avicenna the chief physician was speaking to Prince Julien, addressing him more quietly and yet more urgently now. "Your Highness… Your father's condition has become much more grave. You must leave us now."

The Prince appeared shocked by his father's sudden seizure; clearly distracted, he apparently forgot Floretta, offered no protest and headed obediently for the door.

The physicians absorbed themselves immediately in their work, lifting the King's body tenderly and placing it once more onto the bed, arranging the limbs with infinite care as if they were the petals of a delicate flower or the wings of an injured butterfly.

Then by contrast they began to massage and to slap the body with an alarming and yet precisely calculated violence, each movement dictated it seemed by professional method. One physician slid his hand slowly about the King's chest as if searching for something he could not find and then, placing his two hands upon it one over the other, proceeded to apply a series of sharp, heavy, rhythmical presses.

Floretta was content to follow the Prince out. The last she saw as they left the darkened bedchamber was the figure of Avicenna advancing upon the King with the syringe his apprentice had brought him.

Once more in the King's sitting room, the Prince and Floretta were greeted by the pathetic whining lump which the King's pet mastiff had become. The pitiful creature attempted half-heartedly to push its way into the bedchamber. When the Prince blocked its way and closed the door, it dropped its heavy mass at the Prince's feet, panting heavily and eyeing them both reproachfully and refusing to move, so that the Prince and Floretta were obliged to step round it.

As Floretta's eyes adjusted once more to the brightness of this pleasant sitting room, she observed that it was no longer deserted as it had been earlier. Rather, it was occupied almost to capacity by a formidable gathering of richly attired people, presumably royal personages, elders of the realm or other notables, though who all these people might actually be she had no idea.

The seats were inviting and promised to be comfortable, but no one reclined or lounged while he waited; every seat was vacant; everyone stood solemnly, expressionless but expectant, the assembly grouped about the room in arcs, representing perhaps family groups or factions, each facing the doorway of the King's bedchamber, so that all eyes had fallen on the Prince and Floretta as they emerged, cold, unmoving eyes which revealed no emotion.

No one spoke, no one inquired as to the King's condition, and the Prince, proffering no information, joined the gathering in their silent waiting. The Prince did not align himself with one of the groups but took up a position on his own, looking deeply troubled. Floretta hovered nearby but, in a desire not to attract attention, tried to avoid standing too close to the Prince. She edged instead closer to Ashvy Parva, the Prince's butler, who was in attendance nearby with certain other of the Prince's servants whom she had seen earlier.

In her deference, Floretta did not allow her eyes to search through the assembly for others she might know. To her immense relief, the eyes of the assembly soon left her and the Prince. She cast her eyes to the floor and began to wonder what was to come, whether the physicians would succeed in reviving the King. She wondered too how it was that the Household had assembled there at this opportune moment; it seemed to her that everyone of any significance must be there; someone must have anticipated the King's seizure and sent word.

The whining of the large dog had grown increasingly annoying in the heavy silence of the crowded room. "The beast must be removed," an authoritative voice announced at length. Floretta glanced up cautiously and saw that the speaker was an elderly but upright gentleman of distinguished bearing and aristocratic countenance. "The beast has no place here now," he continued. "It must be removed to the kennels and cared for there."

Floretta looked at him politely as he spoke and suddenly grew aware that standing immediately at his side was a young man she already knew and whom she had been hoping not to meet – the Prince Elbert. The distinguished gentleman could only be his father, the Duke of Ferrar. Then Floretta realised that Elbert in his turn was aware of her presence; he recognised her; his eyes were upon her, and, it seemed, coldly.

The eyes of the two met for an instant and Floretta attempted to avoid his gaze, as meanwhile the servants applied themselves to the task of removing the languid moaning mass of the unwanted mastiff. The beast protested, it would not walk, would not be dragged, but they succeeded at length in carrying it. The poor animal had lost all its dignity. Noticing that Prince Elbert's eyes had been momentarily distracted from her, Floretta slipped further to the side and attempted to conceal herself behind Ashvy Parva and his assistants.

The silence and waiting were now easier to bear, and a considerable length of time passed before the door of the King's bedchamber finally opened and Karezza Avicenna emerged.

"My good lords," he said. "And my gentle ladies. I must announce that our dear king is dead."

"The King is dead," everyone repeated in solemn unison. But no one moved to declare 'Long live the King!'; no one paid homage to Julien. Neither did Julien move to kneel before some other.

There was but one movement in the room; one person and one only stepped forward, a person quite unrecognised by Floretta. He strode across the room towards the grand fireplace and took possession of the richly jewelled sceptre suspended above it. He lifted it over his head with both hands and everyone cheered. "As Lord Chancellor of this realm," he declared, "personally selected by our departing monarch, it falls to me and me alone to pass on the Staff of Majesty according to his wishes. I ask you now, who is the trusted Keeper of His Majesty's Testament?"

"I am that Keeper!"

"Then make yourself known!"

The speaker stepped forward.

"You are the Keeper of the Testament, signed and sealed by His Majesty in the presence of His Majesty's Council?"

"I am that Keeper!"

"Does the Council acknowledge this Keeper? Will all members in agreement say, 'Aye'?"

"Aye!" The agreement appeared universal.

The Lord Chancellor tapped three times with the Staff upon the floor, and then the Keeper of the Testament moved forward and joined him, brandishing a sealed scroll.

"Let all who respect not the will of our departed sovereign remove themselves from this assembly forthwith!" declared the Lord Chancellor.

No one moved or spoke and everyone waited patiently as the Lord Chancellor and the Keeper of the Testament turned proudly about and surveyed each person accusingly.

"All who are present are loyal!" declared the Lord Chancellor at length. "Let us then hear the Dispensation of our Respected Monarch!"

"Thus spake the King!" The Keeper of the Testament broke the seal and unrolled his scroll with a dramatic flourish and read aloud: "I, King Justin XI, sovereign of the lands of Torquella, Ferrar and Bante, hereby bequeath the Staff of Majesty to my brother, Ivan Bartholomew, Grand Duke of Ferrar, that he may bear its responsibility on my death or in my absence as Regent of these lands, until such time as my only son, Julien Elazar, has, in the opinion of my brother and his chosen Lord Chancellor, reached a greater maturity so that he instead may ascend to the Throne in his position as rightful monarch."

The Testament was complete. "Long live the Regent!" echoed the assembly.

The Lord Chancellor moved forward and handed the Staff of Majesty to the Duke of Ferrar, and then fell upon one knee and kissed the new Regent's hand. Now all turned this way and gradually everyone began to kneel, some readily and willingly, others not quite so enthusiastically, a few almost reluctantly. Floretta saw that at length even the good Ashvy Parva fell on his knee and lowered his eyes, and so she too quickly followed suit. One person alone remained aloof and refused to demonstrate allegiance to the new Regent.

"I would speak with you, good Uncle Ferrar," declared the Crown Prince pointedly, upright and proud. "I would make my position clear, though not before the Council or the Servants of the Realm."

"Just so," replied the Regent coldly. "If you must attack me with words, then let us be discreet. Let all who are not of the royal blood withdraw from this chamber."

A large number of those present, including the Lord Chancellor and the Keeper of the Testament, now rose and began to leave. As ever taking Ashvy Parva as her example, Floretta realised that she too would be expected to withdraw and quickly began to follow.

"My servants may remain," stated Prince Julien. His servants at once stood still, awaiting the Regent's word on this.

"Very well," conceded the Regent. "I assume that otherwise you imagine to feel unsafe with me." The Prince's entourage now resumed their kneeling positions.

When all who were excluded had gone, the Regent gestured that all might now stand. "Well, my young nephew?" he inquired.

"My opinion is already known to you personally," stated Julien, "and to others present, but it is my desire that all here now should know my mind. Without question, you have no good claim to the throne of this land."

"My dear nephew," interrupted the Regent. "Do you doubt the authenticity of the document that has just been read to us? You should then have spoken out earlier."

"That it was writ by my father's hand I doubt not," replied Julien. "That is not the matter in question. We need rather ask how it was that my good father ever penned such an obscene document."

"Nephew, it is not for you to question how your father arrived at his decisions!" rebuked the Regent. "Nor even to criticise them. It is for you to respect your father's will, however contrary it may be to your own!"

"How can I respect this will?" declared Julien. "And how can anyone else present? We all doubt its validity. All who show allegiance to you do so through fear, not respect."

"Nephew, you delude yourself. I have the support of the entire family."

"The support of their tongues, Uncle, not of their hearts, remember that! And the tide will turn, for I can confirm what many only suspect: that you deliberately and calculatingly turned my father's mind in his old age and schemed so that you and your heirs might ascend."

"Oh, come come now, dear boy!" scoffed the Regent. "Must your muddled head forever produce such fantasies?"

The Prince ignored this gibe. "It seems," he continued, "that, for the moment at least, your schemes have succeeded. You are well pleased. You have discredited me in the eyes of my father and now apply yourself to undermining my standing in the eyes of the Household."

"My dear boy," interrupted the Regent. "You discredit yourself daily, and do so now. But must I suffer the embarrassment of your taunts before the younger members of our family and in the presence of your lowly servants? Must I allow myself to be thus misused? I suffer your insults simply because I know they can do my standing no harm. All gathered here know only too well that it is you who have always sought to discredit us, myself and my heirs, rather than the converse!"

"Nonsense, Uncle!" snapped the Prince. "Until his illness, my father recognised my worth and so did the entire Royal Household! And despite his rejection of me, throughout this trying time, none has cared for him more than I. Everyone knows that even now I was doing my utmost for him, fighting alongside him for his life, seeking new physicians and nurses, bringing fresh hope…"

"That you have haunted his bedside we doubt not," replied the Regent drily. "We need only ask, with what motive. The sole reply is that the motive was self. Your behaviour is always for self. We all know this.

You lavished your father with attention during his last months solely in a vain attempt to regain his trust, solely to ingratiate yourself!"

"How dare you thus malign me!" exclaimed the Prince. "I am first in succession in this land, not you! Mine is the Supremacy!"

"Not yet, dear nephew," answered the Regent. "As yet, you are far from Supreme. At present, I approach that quality more closely than any other in this realm. I have acquired it through careful study of my brother during his reign and from the example of our good father before that. Both these good kings were born with Supremacy upon them, it shone from their faces, but you Julien, you have always lacked it, and before you will be king, you must acquire it!"

The Regent appeared to be gaining the upper hand in the argument; the Prince's face reflected a terrible anger, but he could offer no reply.

"Your audience is now at an end," concluded the Regent. "I have endured enough of your arrogance and insults. Before we speak again, you must learn to respect me, as does the rest of the family. Only then will you begin to gain their esteem...

"We will meet again this evening in the Throne Room," the Regent continued, "when we will appear together on the balcony facing the square and announce the Regency to the people. In the meantime, the death of my dear brother the King will be made known throughout the land by the lowering of all flags and tolling of all bells. Until this evening, I request you to remain in your apartments. I suggest you devote some time to composing yourself before our meeting so that you may display yourself before the people with dignity."

On this note the Regent turned and swept towards the outer door, and the whole royal family followed. The Prince hurled no further insults after his uncle, whether through prudence or impotence of tongue it could not be known. Even after all had gone, he found no appropriate verbal expression of his anger; wearily, he seated himself before the fire and hid his face in his hands, as if overcome by despair, while his servants hovered helplessly about him, not daring to address him.

Shortly, there came a loud knock upon the door and straightway entered the eight men-at-arms who had until then kept guard without. They saluted their Prince and the officer bowed. "With all respect, Your Highness," he announced. "It was the wish of the Regent that we escort you to your apartments immediately, in the company of any other persons here assembled with you."

CHAPTER 23

Prince Julien voiced no complaint and allowed himself to be escorted to his apartments. He retired into his thoughts and offered no comment on the matter, as if he had quite expected the company of a military guard.

Once in his own rooms, he dismissed his attendants. "Remember all that I have told you in the past," he enjoined them before they left. "Today especially, your behaviour must be discreet and circumspect; you can expect to be followed and watched at all times. So you must make no mention of any of my secret affairs, even to each other." He received their assurances.

Floretta made up her mind at that moment that whenever Parva was dismissed – as he must eventually be – she would take the opportunity to follow him out and leave too. Now that the King had passed away, there seemed no further reason for her to be there and, moreover, she had no wish to be left alone with the Prince, not that she really feared him. But constant adaptation to his many moods had proved taxing, and she had had quite enough. In any case, he had clearly lost interest in her and it seemed appropriate to slip away. She had after all no desire to stay forever.

She would follow Parva from the room, presumably in the first instance to the servant's quarters, even though the Prince's apartments were undoubtedly far grander and much more comfortable. The less demanding company offered by Parva's reliable, steady nature, his apparent lack of emotion, would provide a much needed breath of fresh air, and he would be able to tell her what arrangements there might be for her to return home.

"And what of you?" the Prince began asking Parva when his servants had completed their small tasks and gone. "Are you confident that you will be able to escape the attention of our adversaries and confirm the arrangements made for this day with those concerned?"

"My Lord…" replied Parva rather more guardedly, apparently much more aware of Floretta's continuing presence than the Prince. "Fortunately, it will not be necessary for me to involve myself in this way. In anticipation of events, I have already taken care to confirm your decisions in the appropriate quarters. I have also made it my business to sift all available information so as to convince myself completely that the loyalty of those immediately involved is quite beyond question."

"Excellent!" praised the Prince. "Quite excellent, Parva. It is most shrewd of you to relieve your person – and mine – of suspicion by these devices. It appears you have now fulfilled your duties towards me for today, and with most gratifying efficiency."

Parva bowed. "Thank you, Your Highness."

"You may expect appropriate rewards."

"Thank you again, Your Highness."

"One thing," added the Prince. "I trust that the confusion which will have gripped the Household today has not been allowed to spread to my kitchens? The dinner arrangements are quite in order?"

"But of course, My Lord," replied Parva. "His Royal Highness need not concern himself with such trivialities."

"Then thank you, Parva, you may leave me now."

Parva bowed politely and turned towards the door, and Floretta also made a move in that direction. She reached the door which Parva opened and, at the last moment, as she was about to pass through, the Prince noticed her.

"One moment," he said. "Where are you going?"

It seemed that Parva heard and saw none of this. He continued on his way, passing through the portal and quietly closing the door after himself.

Faced with a closed door and yet resolving not to be outdone, Floretta turned and curtseyed politely to the Prince. It seemed to her that if she were quick she might still be able to catch Parva. "Your Highness, is there anything more I can do for you?" she asked. "I assumed my services were no longer required. I thought perhaps I should return home now for today…"

Return home. Suddenly her heart sank. How she longed to return home! But, she realised at that moment, she could not leave without the flower. That was why she had come – for the flower. She recalled how she had recovered possession of it – and placed it lovingly in sunlight – but then in the confusion had deserted it. She comforted herself with the thought that she did at least know exactly where it was: it was surely standing on the window ledge of the King's bedchamber, exactly where she had left it. But that now seemed a million miles away, for if she could not reach it and tend it soon, it would surely die.

She waited on the Prince's word, but he did not seem to be paying her any attention. He appeared distracted and began to pace the room restlessly. Eventually he replied, "You might still be able to assist me... if you so desire... So I would like you to remain a little longer. But if you are troubled by a need for rest or refreshment, speak out, for those can easily be arranged..."

She shook her head.

"No?" he said. "Well, do at least seat yourself. Ours may be a long wait." He himself sat down.

Floretta followed his example and sank back into a chair, while he sank deeper into his thoughts. She realised sadly that she could not hope to manipulate this Prince; he had time merely for his own troubles, not that she could really expect him to bother himself with hers. She was now beginning to feel very tired and disconsolate. She regretted not having taken the opportunity to ask for something when invited to do so – such as the flower – or someone – such as Parva, who now seemed the only saviour she might have.

"Tell me," he asked at length. "Have you ever had occasion to meet my cousin, the Prince Elbert?"

"Yes," she replied.

"Ahh! And where might that have been?"

"On the market place, Your Highness," she told him. "One market day..."

"I rather fancied as much," he replied triumphantly, not bothering to elicit the whole story from her. "Thank you, you have helped me a great deal."

Floretta could not see how, but the Prince certainly did seem to grow more relaxed after this. He did not engage her in further conversation however and seemed content merely to wait, though for what, she could not imagine.

Considerably later, a rather impudent knock came suddenly upon the door; the doors flew open and, to Floretta's amazement and dismay, in strode the young figure of none other than the Prince Elbert.

"What ho, cousin?" demanded Prince Julien with surprising jocularity. "You desire to see me so eagerly that you invite yourself unannounced into my private chambers?"

Prince Elbert bowed somewhat ostentatiously. "Forgive my intrusion, dear cousin." He smiled. "I will not trouble you long. I found no butler without to announce me, merely a few guards, and I failed to bring along my own for the purpose... I merely wished to inquire as to the identity of the young lady in whose company we see you today."

"Indeed?" replied Julien. "You inquire about the company I keep? On what pretext, I cannot imagine! Have you been appointed my keeper? As for the young lady, her identity is no concern of yours. All that can possibly concern you is that she is at present in the employment of this household as nurse!"

"A nurse?" remarked Elbert. "My dear cousin, how touching! Are you ill? Since when has it been good form for a member of the Royal Line to entertain young nurses in his private apartments?"

"Tut, tut, cousin Elbert," chided Prince Julien. "She is here under the instructions of your father, who I understand is now highest judge in this land! You question his authority? If you remember, I was entreated by him to assemble my retinue here. Most of my servants have now returned to their quarters, but this young lady remains as yet uncatered for. She cannot lodge with the housemaids – she is above their rank – and yet cannot reside with the physicians. As she is the first female nurse to enter my employ, my butler is at this moment arranging a special apartment for her."

"Capital!" declared Elbert. "A female nurse! A splendid innovation indeed! Her presence in this house will be of great assistance. I hope you will not be annoyed if, on occasions, others avail themselves of her services?"

"Not at all," replied Julien.

"Thank you, cousin. That is most noble of you," continued Elbert. "I myself am especially liable to request that she attend my wife, your dear sister the Princess Lilibelle, who as we all know is so prone to pains in the head… In fact, could the young lady perhaps assist me in such wise now?"

"Certainly," replied Julien with considerable magnanimity, rather to Floretta's surprise. "By all means take the young lady. She can retire to her apartment after attending Lilibelle. My butler should arrive soon to escort her to her apartment – I shall refer him on to you."

It was agreed, and so, much to her consternation, Floretta left the Crown Prince's apartments in the company of Prince Elbert.

CHAPTER 24

Prince Elbert did not speak to Floretta until they were alone behind closed doors and had apparently reached their destination. He laughed, rather triumphantly. "My good cousin Julien must be hatching some plot," he told Floretta cheerfully, "to have allowed me to take you from him so easily, for he cares little about the health of Princess Lilibelle, though she is his sister."

"Where is the Princess Lilibelle?" asked Floretta. "Is she resting here in one of these chambers?"

"No," smiled the Prince.

"Then she will arrive soon, I expect," said Floretta.

"No," repeated the Prince.

"Then I misunderstand…"

The Prince looked at Floretta closely and then shook his head as if amazed by her. "How naïve you are," he told her kindly. "How innocent and how gentle. The Princess Lilibelle is not ill! That was merely a ruse, a trick I employed to release you from the clutches of my cousin! I am not taking you to visit the Princess. Surely you know why I came to Julien's apartment, for no other reason than to seek you out. You must know you are the object of my most ardent desires." He knelt before Floretta, and, taking her hand, began to kiss it tenderly.

"Oh," murmured Floretta with surprise.

"Since our first magical meeting in the market place," he told her, "I have not ceased to long for you, to yearn for you, to dream of you. I thought that my imagination had invented you, that you were gone forever. But now you have reappeared, you are real! And you are even lovelier than I remembered! Never has such an angel graced this palace before!

"Your beauty outclasses all other. You can have no rival for my heart; your loveliness is sublime. Why, even the lovely Marianna, brought from her father's kingdom to marry Julien, her beauty is as nothing beside yours! Marianna, who hides herself in her apartments through dislike of the stares her loveliness attracts! She need no longer fear the attention of the eyes of this kingdom…"

"You speak of Prince Julien's wife," said Floretta. "That is strange. Are you not yourself already betrothed? To the Princess Lilibelle…"

"That is so," admitted Elbert. "But there is no love between us and never has been. She is a tiresome, unattractive creature, completely lacking in charm or talent. Why, in comparison, her uninspiring brother Julien even strikes a handsome figure! No, it was a political match, arranged by our fathers and not desired by ourselves and not destined to last. And, now that my father is regent, I suspect that he will wish me to divorce her, for every day her branch of the family sinks into greater disrepute as Julien continues to disgrace himself..."

Prince Julien again! Prince Elbert seemed unable to forget his cousin. "Your dislike for your cousin appears very strong," murmured Floretta. At the back of her mind lurked the suspicion that part at least of Elbert's desire to gain possession of her stemmed from a wish to outdo Julien. How quickly her mind was becoming attuned to the dark undercurrents of Palace life.

"Yes, yes," he replied almost impatiently. "There is little love between my cousin and myself. But let us forget these tedious Affairs of State and think only of ourselves, of my love for you, of our future together... Let us think back to that first day in the market place, that fateful day which holds for me happy and sad memories, so closely interwoven, of how I first became enchanted by you and declared my love... I see now, that on that occasion I surprised you with my ardour, I overwhelmed you, I shocked you... I gave you no chance to reflect, no time to consider... But I am sure you have since had all the time you need to regret your hasty refusal, and so we can put that sadness behind us and look instead forward, to our joyful future..."

"You are going to be my queen!" he declared. "Majesty will come easily to you; you are already possessed of a simple regality. It will not be long now before my father is king. He is arranging with his ministers for Julien to be disinherited, and so, you see, in time, the Throne will pass to me! By then I will no longer be troubled by Lilibelle so that you alone will share my throne with me..."

Floretta was horrified by these revelations but dared not speak her mind; she was learning that there was great danger in being too frank with a prince. But likewise, she sensed the danger of not speaking out and thereby encouraging Elbert further. It came as something of a relief to her to hear a knock upon the door.

"Come in!" called the Prince, drawing back from Floretta, pulling himself upright and straightening his clothing guiltily.

The door opened to reveal one servant who seemed reluctant to enter.

"So it is you, is it, Ofan?" rebuked the Prince. "I am surprised that you trouble me now. Are you not informed that I am engaged in important business? What matter can be of such great importance that it warrants this disturbance?"

"I am deeply sorry, Your Highness," replied the servant, "but Her Ladyship insisted that I bring the message that she requires to see you immediately in her apartments."

"You may tell Her Ladyship," instructed the Prince, "that for Affairs of State she must wait, and that if time allows I will come later."

"So be it, Your Highness." The servant bowed and hurriedly took his leave.

"Please forgive that interruption, my dear," Elbert told Floretta. "Thus may it be for some months, I fear. But fortunately you will be residing in the Palace and we shall be able to see each other as frequently as we wish during this trying time of waiting before we can belong to each other."

"Alas," said Floretta. "I was not intending to reside in the Palace for long. I was engaged merely to attend His Majesty the King, and now that he is deceased…"

"That produces no problem," Elbert reassured her. "It will be a simple matter to obtain a more permanent position for you, a position which, it goes without saying, I shall ensure is not too strenuous."

"But you misunderstand," she insisted. "I do not wish to live at the Palace. My mother has not always been well and she needs me very much and I do so wish to go home to her."

"Do not allow that to trouble you," he said. "In a large household like this, it will be elementary to arrange lodging for your mother too."

"You cannot persuade me," she blurted. "I have no desire to stay. I long to go home to my cottage so much. I feel so out of place in a palace, so lost…"

Elbert was not angry; he appeared deeply concerned. "It had not crossed my mind," he said, "that you might feel strange here." He took her hand again. "What can I do to make things easier for you?" he asked, looking with sincerity into her eyes. "If you do not tell me, I cannot know. You must speak up, if there is anything in my power which can be done for you."

Tears came to Floretta's eyes in response to this show of kindness. "There is nothing you can possibly do for me," she sniffed. "It would be many years indeed before I could feel at all at home in a palace. You see,

I do not like to be closed in. I like to be in the open air, to be out in the forest, to be living with the countryside…"

"Then I will build you a garden!" he exclaimed. "With your favourite trees, and all your favourite flowers!"

Floretta was moved by his generosity, encouraged to trust him, and at the same time tempted. Might she ask the Prince to bring her her special flower? Would it be wrong to use her influence over him in this way? She decided not. After all, the flower was rightfully hers.

"You have guessed correctly," she told him, "that I love flowers. In fact, that is how my name was chosen: Floretta."

"Floretta," he breathed. "My little flower…"

"I have always loved to tend flowers," she explained. "Especially the forest flowers. It hurts me to see them crushed or dying. There was a flower I saw today that tore at my heart. It was a flower taken from the forest that had been terribly neglected. But I believe it was not quite dead…"

"Floretta," he insisted. "You need only speak your wishes. This flower, tell me where!"

"It was on the window ledge of the King's bedchamber," she replied. "A pathetic withered stump which no one would cherish but I…"

"I will send at once for it!" he told her as he rushed to the door. She was aware of hurried instructions being issued in the corridor and then he returned to her. "What else can I bring you, my dear gentle one?" he implored. "What else that will bring a smile to your lips and a twinkle to your eyes? Speak out! If one flower brings you joy, then tomorrow I will send you a million selected scented blooms!"

"You are too kind," she told him. "I do not need a million flowers."

"Nonsense," he assured her gently. "Your happiness is as my own. Express your every wish and it will be granted! You will be my queen, we can be sure of that, but you will not be my unhappy queen! My queen must be filled with joy!"

So still the Prince did not understand. A sense of helplessness gripped Floretta. She felt drained of energy. She knew she could achieve no more that day. Her tears began to flow more readily.

"Please forgive me, Your Highness," she asked, "that I seem so ungrateful. But I am so tired and can think of no way to repay your kindness…" She remembered rising that morning with the sun. It seemed so long ago. She remembered the injuries from which she was only just recovering. She recalled her journey, her arrival at the Palace, the many surprises and lessons of the day. Had all this happened in one day? It had. And, now that the sun was beginning to set again, she longed for the safety of her little bed. She must sleep soon, in any bed. She would make everything clear to the Prince in the morning…

"You must retire now, my dear one," Elbert was telling her. "I must send you to your room. I can see that you are suffering greatly from fatigue. And I suspect you have not been well…"

He rose from Floretta's side and gazed hopefully at the door. "Oh, Ashvy Parva!" he cursed. "Where is that man? Always so unreliable if his business does not directly benefit Julien!"

He paced up and down. "Floretta," he continued at length. "If the butler does not come soon with news of your apartment, I must leave you here. My presence is required in the Throne Room very shortly, and I must prepare myself."

The Prince seemed pleased when this time a knock came at the door. "Ah! That will be Parva now," he declared. But it was not. "Do you bring word from Ashvy Parva or Prince Julien?" he asked the caller.

"No, Your Highness, I do not," came the reply. "I bear an important message from the Duke of Ferrar. His personal messenger declared to me that, by your father's word, your presence is no longer required in the Throne Room this evening. I was requested to emphasise that in no circumstance were you to attend."

"Thank you, my man, you may go," replied the Prince. "Or rather, just one minute! While you are here you may assist me in another matter. I have a message to be delivered. Find Prince Julien's butler, Ashvy Parva, and inform him that I would speak with him immediately."

Elbert closed the door once more. "How very odd," he muttered to himself. "I cannot understand it. What can my father be about?"

Floretta was falling asleep now on the Prince's sofa, her eyes still wet with her tears.

"You cannot be comfortable there, my dear," he murmured. "Perhaps you should rest awhile on my bed."

Floretta allowed herself to be led through into Elbert's bedchamber. His bed was unbelievably soft and soothing as the resilient moss of the forest. It welcomed Floretta and caressed her. Elbert gave her one kiss. "Sleep soundly, dearest one," he whispered to her as he left.

But then he returned and woke her again and once more she cried, but this time her tears were warm tears of joy, for he had brought her her beloved flower. As her tears fell onto it, so the flower appeared grateful and refreshed and seemed to reawaken to a new vigour, while she herself sank ever deeper into a welcome sleep.

CHAPTER 25

While Floretta slept she dreamed at first of Elbert and of his professed love for her. Each image and recollection was tinged with wonder, for in her young life she had had no experience of the love between man and woman. And then her heart reached out towards the only person she herself had ever deeply loved, the only person she had ever known well enough to have learned to cherish; she fancied that she was with her old grandmother, and then her mother, again.

The fancy grew stronger, and Floretta's spirit freed itself from the point where it was locked and drifted out of the Palace, seeking that place she knew as home. But before she had gone far she had found her mother. She arrived at her mother's side quickly and hovered so close she could touch her, she could kiss her. Her mother was really there. Floretta was with her; and yet she was not.

She sensed that her mother was worried about her; her mother had headed for town in the hope of gaining news. And yet she could not make her mother aware that she was there; she seemed unable to hear Floretta when she spoke, did not turn when Floretta tugged at her sleeve. Floretta grew angry that her mother would not listen to the reassurances she offered. She had no suspicion that she had drifted there only in spirit.

Flora was arriving in the market place. Indeed, everyone seemed to be flocking to the market place: the whole town was abroad. But not because there was a market. It was too late in the day for that. It was evening and the sun was setting, casting dark, crimson shadows across the heavy clouds which quarrelled in the turbulent sky. The day had been pleasant, rather warm, and now there promised to be thunder. The heat of the day remained locked beneath the oppressive clouds, so that jostling with the restive crowd which was thronging the market square was not the most agreeable way to spend the evening. The crowd was growing impatient, and many were beginning to hope for the blessing of a light rain.

Floretta could not imagine why the crowd was there. If only her mother would speak to her, if only she could reassure her… Her mother would not stand still even for one moment.

The square was overfull and Flora hung behind the others. The people were backed against the commercial premises that flanked the sides of the square, the more agile clambering up the façades to obtain a better view. Everyone avoided the unfenced river on the eastern edge.

The square was in growing darkness as night fell – apart from the flaming torches brandished by the more adventurous and festive of the crowd – but the Palace was lit up from within; the curtains were not drawn on the first floor and all the lights shone out brightly into the dusk so that the Palace appeared as a jewelled diadem set against the royal colour of the sky.

The Palace! Everyone was facing the Palace! Floretta remembered now where she should be and in sudden panic her spirit fled from her mother's side and span through the heavy air towards the bright lights. Even as she returned, the crowd surged up, though through no response to her, it seemed; the crowd rose and cheered to acknowledge the end of their wait as a figure appeared on the illuminated balcony above the central portal. But then, among the cheering, there came jeers and, as Floretta sped above the heads of the crowd towards the Palace, she saw that some fists were shaken. The figure on the balcony raised his hands as if requesting quiet. And then, even as Floretta arrived immediately before the bright lights, the figure contorted and crumpled. It slipped down and lay on the stone slabs of the balcony below Floretta's eyes. Its chest had been pierced by some sort of projectile and it was rapidly becoming covered in its own blood.

Overcome with horror, Floretta's spirit shot up and away and, as her mind screamed, her consciousness merged with the blood red of the sunset sky. She span about in confusion and saw that down in the square below all was turmoil too; the people surged hither and thither screaming, panicking for cover, but few finding any. Floretta had lost sight of the small figure of her mother. And now red-coated men-at-arms came swarming from the Palace outbuildings and out through the gates, pushing aside the people and forcing entry into the businesses on the southern side of the square. Floretta had no place there any longer; she was thankful to regain the peace of her own body once more.

* * * * *

Almost immediately, Floretta was woken from her troubled sleep. At first she could not recollect where she was; she had never slept in a strange bed away from home before. The dark shapes of this large room were quite unknown to her. The room was not in complete darkness, for the curtains were drawn back and it was partially light outside. The sky cast a crepuscular glow which provided the meagre illumination of the room. Whether this was the dim light of early dawn or the fading low rays of dusk, indeed, how long she might have slept, Floretta had no way of knowing.

Nonetheless, recognising the chamber at last and remembering where she was, her thoughts turned to why she had woken. For the moment, the memory of her ugly dream eluded her. She knew only that she had been roused by the sounds of bitter crying from the direction of Prince Elbert's sitting room. The anguish in the high-pitched voices tugged at her heart. Unable to distinguish the words from where she lay, she slipped out of bed and, finding she shivered, dragged the counterpane after her to wrap about herself. She crept to the door and attempted to overhear the rush of conversation beyond. But she was still unable to hear properly and, observing that the door was not fully shut, yielded to the temptation of pulling it open a crack. She could now hear clearly, and she could see.

Luckily for her, the group of people without were too preoccupied to notice her action or to suspect she was there. Floretta saw Prince Elbert and three others. The Prince was seated on his sofa, his face stricken white and his expression dazed. He gripped his arms tightly and protectively about two little girls who were kneeling close before him, clutching at him desperately for support, crying almost hysterically as if beside themselves with grief. The other figure was a handsome young boy who resembled Elbert rather strongly, it seemed to Floretta, and who was standing there recounting to Elbert a long and bitter tale.

"It was awful," he was telling Elbert. "Everybody was absolutely terrified."

"I didn't like the screaming," cried the smaller of the two girls.

"The screaming?" questioned Elbert.

"Yes," the young boy confirmed. "There was so much of it. Everybody was at it and it went on and on. When the crowd started screaming outside, everyone inside started screaming too. They screamed and backed against the walls, though I don't suppose at that stage they had any idea what had happened – I didn't, anyway – just that something terrible was going on."

"No, I didn't know what was happening," said the larger of the two girls. "I was screaming just because everybody else was."

"Yes, it was everybody else," said the smaller girl. "The grown-up ladies started me off. They made me scream even more…"

"At first no one dared go out to Father," continued the young boy, whom Floretta now saw to be Elbert's brother. "I suppose they were frightened the same thing might happen to them, which in the circumstances was reasonable enough, I suppose… But eventually some of the men carried Father in. It was awful. I told the little ones not to look, but myself I couldn't look away. I had to look because otherwise I wouldn't have believed it. He was covered in blood, but somehow he was still breathing, even though the blood was pumping from his chest… They didn't seem to know what to do about it…"

Floretta's forgotten dream returned to her in a flash. So what she had dreamt had actually happened?

"…Someone said it had been done with a crossbow – there was no other possibility – and the men agreed it was a very good shot. They kept on that whoever had done it must be a very good marksman. But they didn't do anything. The only person that didn't just stand there was Julien: he insisted on talking to Father, asking him which direction it had come from."

"Did Father reply?" asked Elbert.

"Yes, even though it pained him so. He attempted to raise his right arm to say it had come from the right. And then I pulled Julien away from him and told him to leave my father alone. He was angry but ignored me, and made great show of sending word to his own personal guard to go forth from the Palace and comb the buildings on that side… I suppose that was a sensible thing to do, although I don't know why he couldn't send the King's Guard… and meanwhile Father was suffering…"

"Did Julien not send for a physician?" asked Elbert.

"The physician had already been summoned, or so it appeared, though I couldn't say by whom. He arrived very promptly. It was Karezza Avicenna. He himself looked very shocked and sent for his assistants, and entreated us all to withdraw to the adjoining chamber. We did not want to leave Father but Avicenna insisted. He would not even allow Mother to remain. But Julien, of course, he did not withdraw. He went instead onto the balcony and addressed the screaming crowd."

"Did he dare?" asked Elbert. "Was he not afraid? So soon after…"

"Yes, he dared," replied the young boy, but there was bitterness in his voice and no admiration for Julien. "But it was no great act of courage because by then his men were swarming everywhere outside."

"But did they listen?" demanded Elbert. "Surely the crowd did not listen?"

"Oh, yes." His brother sounded very sour. "Yes, they did. They silenced themselves obediently and paid attention to him. Yes, they listened to him, even though they had not listened to Father…"

"So they acknowledged him," said Elbert. "And what did he say to them? Did you hear?"

"Yes, we heard him. When the noise of the crowd abated, we in the next chamber moved to the windows and peeped out and attempted to quieten our mourning on seeing he was about to speak."

"How spoke he then?"

"He said, he said…" The young boy was finding increasing difficulty in speaking. "He said that, that the Duke of Ferrar would not be able to address them that evening as planned, and that they were to return straightway to the safety of their homes. He told them that, if they would reassemble tomorrow at noon, he himself would address them and would inform them as to the condition of the Duke. And then the crowd began to disperse, once more noisily."

"He said no more?" asked Elbert. "He offered no insults to our father's person?"

The young boy shook his head. "He was very cool," he replied, sounding almost regretful. "He came through to the chamber where we were all assembled after that. And although the ladies were crying and all the men were shocked and agitated, he himself seemed above the situation…"

"And then the Council arrived," he went on, "the whole Council. Though by whose convocation I know not. It appears that they had gained word of the crisis and had delivered themselves accordingly. And then, and then, Karezza Avicenna came through from the Throne Room." Elbert's young brother now began to cry along with his sisters. "And announced, announced the death, of, of our father the Regent."

"And Julien? What did Julien do?" asked Elbert urgently.

"He did nothing. He just stood there. And then the Lord Chancellor made a speech. He said how very much he regretted having to perform such duties twice in one day, and then he announced what I was fearing, that the Throne could pass only to the first in succession in the land. He cried 'Long live the King' and the rest of the Council, and the family, echoed him, though I myself did not join in, I swear! Then he knelt before Julien and kissed his hand! And then everyone knelt."

"Everyone?" asked Elbert incredulously. "Everyone knelt?"

"Yes," sobbed his brother bitterly. "Everyone. Just as they did this same day to Father!"

"If I had been there, I would not have knelt," declared Elbert. "For my father would never have so degraded himself."

"But you were not there," accused his brother.

"Yes, why weren't you there?" sobbed the little ones. "We missed you… We needed you…"

"But Father requested me not to attend!" insisted Elbert.

"How so?" asked his brother querulously. "He mentioned naught of it to me."

"I received a message…" Elbert declared, "from his own lips… It may well be that he had received intelligence as to the possibility of an attack and wished at least to ensure my safety…"

"That must be what happened," replied his brother. "What a courageous man our dear father shows himself to have been, still to face the people in such dangerous circumstances… So will I remember him." He began to sob again. "But I still wish that you had been there, Elbert, to give me courage, for I knelt before Julien… I confess it to you now. If you had been with me, then I would not have done so, I swear it. I showed myself most reluctant, but Mother pulled me down when she saw that I hesitated and muttered to me that it was dangerous not to kneel…"

"Good brother, you must not blame yourself," Elbert reassured him. "I am confident that your behaviour was most correct."

"After this, the family began to disperse. Before leaving, everyone came and offered Mother their sympathy and she began to cry once more. She wanted to go through to see Father, she could not believe that he was dead, but Avicenna prevented her…"

"And then…" sobbed the larger of the little girls. "And then… we just couldn't bear it any longer and ran away and came looking for you."

"Yes," agreed their brother. "We came looking for you. Or rather, they came first and I felt obliged to follow, to take care of them. I was rather unwilling to leave Mother, but the physician appeared to be attending her, and I felt sure she would be safe in his care… Tell me, brother," he asked. "What happens now? Can we allow this situation?"

"What happens now," repeated Elbert. "What happens now indeed. Do we allow this situation or can we change it? Either nothing happens or else everything. Either we acknowledge the accession of Julien or else we fight it. But before we decide to fight, we must be sure we can win. There could be no capitulation, no compromise. For it is the middle road between the two directions we could take which would lead to the greatest danger. I see now how it was that I received that fateful message from Father, though I doubt now that it can have been from his lips. It would appear that Julien anticipated my opposition and sent it himself to ensure my absence. For I would have been the flaw in his plans, the flicker to kindle his rejection by the whole family."

"You imply," said his brother quietly, "that Julien had foreknowledge of our father's assassination."

"Yes," Elbert replied, "I do imply that. But we could never gain the information to prove it."

CHAPTER 26

On hearing the arrival of other persons, Floretta hurriedly drew back from the door. She hoped that the ladies who had at that moment entered had not noticed her, though through no feeling of guilt at her eavesdropping, no fear of reprimand. She merely did not wish to intrude her presence into their affairs and had no desire to become drawn into the conversation. It was not for her to concern herself with Affairs of State; she felt she should remain apart.

Not only had present affairs shown themselves to be ugly and complicated beyond her previous experience, she also found herself powerless to decide where her allegiance lay. Having acquired her knowledge of the situation from so many different angles, she had gained no clear concept of the truth. One thing only could she be sure of: that the hatred which seared the royal family was reciprocated in both directions. She could not begin to guess to what extent this hatred might be warranted, could only speculate as to who the original architect of the situation might have been.

However, she did not wish to cut herself off completely from the tide of events and so still she trained her ear towards the door. For, only by gaining greater knowledge could she come to understand more clearly the disharmony which appeared to characterise the World of Man.

The children had largely subdued their crying now, especially since the arrival of the group of women, so that it had become easier to follow the thread of conversation through the heavy door.

"Mother, I am pleased you are here," Elbert was saying, "but you must not allow yourself to speak to me of the events of the day, as you will only distress yourself further. The children have told me everything. I think perhaps it would be better for you to retire now."

"Do not concern yourself for me, dear son." The voice sounded that of a sensitive, affectionate woman. "For I am much recovered now. The physician has given me a calmative and so I hope I will now be able to remain in the forefront of events. I have no wish to retire while so much is still at stake."

"I appreciate your support, Mother," Elbert replied, "but you must leave everything to me. I must show myself strong enough to handle the situation on my own."

"I wish you luck in your stand," she replied, "but allow me to warn you, dear son: be on guard, for I suspect our new would-be king is already planning some mischief in your direction. Even as I departed from my consultation with the good physician, I fancied I saw Julien's minions very much at large in the corridors, carrying messages hither and thither to convoke the family once again or arrange some other such business…"

Even as she spoke, the sounds of a large body of people could be heard moving in their direction along the corridor outside.

"Well, how little time he allows for mourning in this household," remarked the Duchess sadly. "Weigh your every word, son," she cautioned again. "Think three times before you speak, or he will trap you with your own words!"

The approaching group paused outside for one second only before entering. The knock to request entry was perfunctory in the extreme. The doors opened straightway and the group entered.

"Pray forgive the intrusion, cousin." Floretta recognised the sarcastic voice of Julien, erstwhile Prince, newly King of Torquella. "I am sad to disturb your family gathering, but as your presence was not noted in the Throne Room earlier this evening, we deemed it our duty to transmit to you news of events which have come to pass there."

"With all respect, cousin, I would request you to speak no more of those awful happenings," replied Elbert coolly, "as I have already received full details from my family here and to reiterate those details before them would serve merely to renew and to heighten their distress."

"Exactly so," answered Julien. "For that very reason would I myself request that your good mother the Duchess withdraw, and that her children and maids-in-waiting depart with her. For the bloody business of the times such as we two must now discuss is most unsuitable for the ears of the gentler sex or of their half-grown pups."

"Elbert, does he mean that I too must go?" demanded the Prince's younger brother. "I will not leave you."

"The presence of any minor is highly inappropriate in view of the special nature of the business in hand," replied Julien in Elbert's place. "So I do suggest that you too, young cousin, leave this assembly. You are not yet man enough to be included in men's affairs."

"Come, dear son," coaxed the Duchess. "For I need a man with me, and for me, you are man enough. Let us leave these larger men to the largeness of their manly deliberations."

Floretta heard the outer doors close once more and presumed that the Duchess and her family had left. There followed an uneasy silence.

At last, Julien spoke. "It is my duty first to bring you formal confirmation of the untimely demise of your good father," he told Elbert. "And to express to you my deepest sympathy for your loss."

"So be it," replied Elbert.

"It is my second duty," continued Julien slowly, "on behalf of those congregated here, to issue a warrant for your arrest and trial." He held up a piece of paper.

"How so, cousin?" demanded Elbert. "In what way have I already offended you in your career as king?"

"On the contrary," Julien informed him coldly. "You have not offended me personally, you have offended the morals of the realm."

"This is preposterous," exclaimed Elbert. "Who has signed this trashy writ you toss before me? And who has prepared it? Any other but yourself?"

"It bears two signatures," replied Julien. "My own, as recognised head of this royal house, plus that of the Lord Chancellor, given amid much sadness and misgiving and only after the most thorough of deliberations with his Council."

"Thorough!?" Elbert retorted. "When can your Council have had any time for 'thorough deliberation' since your hasty accession?"

"The same Council which served my father and yours has been in constant discussion all this day," answered Julien. "And during the later hours, their deliberations have centred upon reports freshly received of your activities. At the same time they have been receiving such witnesses as have been available to present themselves."

"This examination of me was then commenced with my father's knowledge and approval?" queried Elbert. "That I very much doubt. How readily, I suspect, you share your wealth with the Servants of the Realm! It seems you have corrupted my father's Council and tried me already, during his administration, in my absence and behind his back!"

Elbert's assertion aroused a murmur of comment.

"Silence!" demanded Julien almost uncertainly. "I must have silence, to inform the detainee of his rights, to assure him that he has not yet been tried!"

"When then will my trial take place?"

"Very shortly, as soon as it can be arranged."

"And what witnesses have you assembled against me?"

"You will have opportunity to examine any of the witnesses brought by the State at your trial," replied Julien. "You will be allowed to conduct a defence and to provide any witnesses of your own that you may find to contradict the evidence."

"Then present me your evidence now that I may prepare my denial of it," demanded Elbert, "and kindly read your worthless warrant and state the charge!"

"Very well," agreed Julien. "Pray read for me, good Chancellor," he asked, "for it grieves me thus to condemn my own kinsman."

"Certainly, My Lord," replied the resonant voice of the Lord Chancellor. "Ahem! We, the undersigned, that is, in the first instance, King Julien I, sovereign of all Torquella, Ferrar and Bante, and, in the second instance, Arnim Bettina, chosen Lord Chancellor of the aforesaid sovereign, are obliged by the pressure of weighty evidence to issue this day a written indictment for the legal arrest and trial of His Royal Highness the Prince Elbert of Ferrar. The indictment will hereafter be referred to as 'this paper'... The custody of the aforenamed defendant..."

"The charge!" demanded Elbert impatiently. "Read the charge!"

"If His Royal Highness will allow me to finish," requested the Lord Chancellor, "or at least somewhat to summarise the document. If that does not conflict with His Majesty's wishes?.."

"Quickly," instructed Julien. "Reach the point quickly."

"Ahem! To summarise, the – ah – stated charge is a most serious one and concerns a most heinous and comparatively rare offence against the morals of the realm..." The Lord Chancellor sounded embarrassed, almost reluctant to continue. "That of congress with a known witch."

Certain of the assembly gasped and a ripple of comment spread around the room; it was obvious that not everyone present had had foreknowledge of the exact substance of the charge.

"'Congress'...?" cried Elbert. "How so, 'congress'? The only 'congress' of which I have partaken has been with my own wife!" But his voice could be heard to waver. "Does..."

He broke off as the outer doors opened and yet another person entered, someone whose gait was other than dainty and whose entry caused a stir.

Raising his voice and speaking with greater self-assurance, Elbert completed his question: "Does His Majesty the King wish to imply that my wife, his own sister, is a 'known witch'?"

"What! What is this?" demanded the newcomer truculently. "What is going on?" The voice was a woman's, but it was not a gentle voice. "Is this how you repay my devotion, Elbert, after having neglected me the whole day, and now that, being no longer able to wait for you, I have lowered myself to seek you out at last?"

"My dear," replied Elbert. "I would have sought out your presence many minutes ago, after concluding an audience with my mother on the occasion of her tragic bereavement, had not your brother, in his first flush of kingship, delayed me with another tiresome attempt to incarcerate me!"

"Indeed?" she asked, addressing herself to Julien. "What fanciful charge do you present this time, brother?"

"Dear Lilibelle," Julien answered coolly. "Now that I am king I would in the first place request you to address me with greater dignity, as is now increasingly appropriate. And, secondly, I would entreat you to remove your presence as the discussion in hand concerns a matter too indelicate for the ears of a lady. I bid you good evening, dear sister."

"No, Julien," she replied. "I will not go. Someone spoke of a 'witch'. Elbert said you had called me a 'witch'! I must know whether that is so. I would know more of your so-called 'indelicate' business. For if my husband really is on trial then I imagine I shall be required to hear the unsavoury details at some juncture!"

"Allow her to stay, and finish the business quickly, cousin," groaned Elbert wearily.

"Very well," Julien grudgingly agreed. "Then, for the benefit of my sister, I must recapitulate that His Royal Highness Prince Elbert is to be tried on the odious charge of 'congress with a known witch'..."

"'Congress'? What do you mean 'congress'?.." began the Princess Lilibelle.

"Be quiet, dear," insisted Elbert, "or you will be asked to leave..."

"As earlier stated," resumed Julien, "the writ was signed following reports on Prince Elbert's activities throughout this day. I am reluctant to reveal details which should be retained for his trial, but it appears I am required to be more explicit... Elbert was seen to enter his apartments – the very apartments where we stand now – in the company of a lascivious young woman who is renowned in the market place and taverns for her carnal behaviour and occult powers..."

At last, Floretta recognised the reference to herself and began to suspect what might be in store. Filled with horror, she began very slowly to back away from the doors which concealed her person from the gathering.

"There are three witnesses prepared to testify as to the status and habits of this young woman," continued Julien, "and no doubt many more could be found if that were deemed necessary. Those who introduced her into this household disguised her as a nurse so that her presence might go unnoticed. They replaced her meretricious attire with more simple garments. And, I feel compelled to admit, I myself regretfully had accidental dealings with her when, shortly before my father's death, I came across her in his bedchamber! Ostensibly, she was there in her capacity as 'nurse'. It became clear to me only later that she had been there for evil purposes…"

"But, may I ask, at whose instigation, Your Majesty?" This self-assured voice was new to Floretta.

"My dear Count," replied Julien. "Surely the answer is on your own lips? At the instigation of none other than Prince Elbert himself and of his now deceased father…"

"That accusation is ludicrous!" cried Elbert. "For you took that young lady there yourself!"

"Be silent, cousin," exclaimed Julien. "Your objection is noted but quite overruled. Consider, for what purpose would I seek to precipitate my beloved father's death? Be silent, as I myself wished to remain. For I did not wish to sully the tradition of this family with a charge of MURDER!!"

Floretta shuddered. Such distortions of reality! Had His Royal Highness taken leave of his senses?

"The actual charge on which my cousin is indicted," continued Julien, "avoids any implication of malevolence within this family. It concerns not so much my father's death, more my cousin's behaviour following it. We seek to forget my cousin's earlier activities and concentrate our attention on his response to today's tragic events. It appears my father's death pleased him, for he did not dismiss the aforesaid witch but brought her here to his chambers to celebrate! Thereafter the two were so busily occupied, it seems, that my cousin quite forgot pressures of state and, alone among the whole family, failed to present himself this evening!"

"I cannot allow you to condemn me like this," stammered Elbert. "For you know that my absence was your doing!"

"Cousin, do not delay us further with obscure counter-accusations," asked Julien. "This business is already too painful…"

"But you know that you have tricked me," complained Elbert, an increasing uncertainty gripping his voice. "You have schemed to place me at your mercy. What do you want of me? Do you wish me to supplicate to you, to humble myself, to cringe and to beg? Well, I cannot, for it is you who planned that I would be here now, you who misled me with a false message, you who provided a girl…"

"What girl?" asked the Princess Lilibelle querulously. "I must say this business grows more and more intriguing. What witch? What girl?"

"Yes, produce the witch," agreed the gathering. "Produce the witch."

"He undoubtedly has her concealed somewhere here about," declared Julien.

At the sound of footsteps heavily approaching her door, Floretta attempted to shrink further away, but her retreat had been blocked by the bed. She crouched there frozen with fear, the counterpane which she still gripped gradually sliding from her, as the doors were flung open wide and she became the object of scrutiny of all the curious eyes without. Never before had so many men stared upon her at once and so accusingly. She began to tremble. Only one pair of female eyes regarded her, and they too lacked any trace of sympathy. Rather, in those hard eyes lay jealousy, hatred, a trace of cruelty and now a tendency to wildness, even to derangement, as their owner began to utter piercing and terrifying screams.

"Of course," Julien was saying, apparently oblivious to this awful noise, "the adultery on its own, committed against the sister of the King, becomes a treasonous offence. Unfaithfulness so early in marriage is quite inexcusable; I knew that my sister would be heartbroken… Bring in the guards! Seize them! Naturally, the witch will be executed as well…"

"Cousin, cousin, answer one last question," begged Elbert as he was seized by the men-at-arms. "Tell me, who will be my judge?"

"Why, cousin, I, of course," replied Julien, "as highest authority in this land."

"Then have mercy on me, I beseech you, have mercy, have mercy…"

CHAPTER 27

Shortly after her arrest in Prince Elbert's apartments, Floretta found herself locked in a rude and comfortless cell: cold, damp, draughty, dark, and furnished only with a makeshift bed, equipped with just one dirty bedcovering. But at least she was used to sleeping in the simplest of wooden cots with a hard straw mattress. She closed her eyes and pretended she was tucked up in her little bed now; she could almost believe it. And then she thought for a few moments of Prince Elbert and of the deliciously soft bed that he was used to and which she herself had sampled. With his refined tastes and delicate sensibilities, he would find imprisonment much more difficult to bear. With these thoughts she had fallen asleep.

Floretta awoke to find bright rays of morning sun greeting her through her high barred window and to discover that already guards had arrived to escort her sad stiff body away. She went with them, not knowing where they were taking her nor for what purpose, but offering no protest.

They climbed the narrow dark stairs down which she had been dragged the previous night; they passed along many of the broad light corridors which to her had become a familiar feature of the Palace; finally they deposited her before a strange door.

"You are to go in there and wait," the guards told her gruffly.

Floretta obediently entered and closed the door behind herself. What she found was no surprise. She was in yet another of the Palace's beautiful private apartments, she knew not whose. She did not recognise it as Julien's nor as his father's, nor even as Elbert's. But it was equally splendid and luxurious. Whose apartment could it be?

Strangely, all the connecting doors had been left wide open, so that it was possible to see straight into the bedroom, the dressing room, the bathroom… Floretta glanced cautiously around. The apartment was obviously a woman's, for the dressing room contained a large selection of women's clothing: dresses, underskirts, corselettes, slippers… But whose were they? Who had sent for Floretta? Had the Duchess of Ferrar succeeded in rescuing her, only to be seized herself and dragged away at the last moment before Floretta arrived? Or had the Princess Lilibelle sent for her, to punish her or even to persecute her? Was she perhaps watching Floretta from some position of concealment that very minute?

Next Floretta found the dining room. Here an inviting meal with warm and cold dishes lay waiting upon the table, as if the owner of the apartment were expected. The table was laid for one. Floretta was hungry and was tempted to eat but dared not.

The dining room was the loveliest room, filled with warm morning sunshine. The large windows looked out onto a peaceful and well-tended garden. Floretta flung open the glazed doors and passed gladly into the fresh air. A fountain played before her, sweetening the air with spray and providing a bathing pool for the little birds. And all around was an abundance of delicately formed, sweet-smelling flowers of all colours, and behind these flower beds were bushes, and behind the bushes trees, then taller trees, and then a high wall. A very high wall. All thought of attempting escape through the garden passed from Floretta.

She returned indoors, crossed the dining room and entered the sitting room again. No one had arrived; nothing had changed. The meal in the dining room was growing cold. Had not the butler been rather remiss in serving it so soon? Would not His – or rather Her – Highness be annoyed to arrive and find their breakfast spoiled? Floretta returned to the main door, hoping to find the solution to the mystery, hoping to meet her host – or rather hostess – and entreat them to hurry.

She opened the doors. The guards outside sprang immediately around; Floretta recoiled. Her way through was blocked first by crossed sabres and beyond that by a formation of sharp bayonets all levelled at her!

"You must stay in there and wait!" she was told by a harsh voice. "You may not leave."

"But, but, the meal!" she stammered.

"Eat it," she was told. "Go in, close the door, take the meal and eat it. And don't come out again!"

* * * * *

Floretta ate some of the food hurriedly, almost guiltily, and still no one came. At length, she began to wish she had washed before eating – she had after all come from a filthy cell – and that she had lingered over the meal. But she had been reluctant to make use of the bathroom when she had arrived, though she had felt tempted by the pitchers of hot and cold water that she had noticed standing waiting.

Now she returned to the bathroom. The hot water was cooling rapidly and would soon go to waste. She decided she should put it to use and started emptying the pitchers into the tub. As she had suspected, there was plenty of warm water, certainly enough for a bath, and she felt she might dare to take one. For soaps and powders and perfumes and clean towels were in extravagant supply and she felt sure that her host – or hostess – would not be offended at her taking this liberty.

She lay long in the bath, savouring the sweet experience, the caress of the soft warm water, the scent of the delicate perfume. When at last she emerged, she reviewed her clothing with disgust, crumpled and soiled by the mire of the cell. And so she borrowed some of her hostess's clothes from the many that decorated the dressing room. All the dresses were very fine: exquisitely designed and expertly worked from the most costly fabrics. They were all about her size. She was loath to try on the very best for fear they were her hostess's personal favourites, and instead selected one of the more modest. But even this dress was so fine that she would never wish to return home in it, and so Floretta set about washing her own clothes.

Return home? Did she really imagine she was about to return home? As she washed her clothes, she realised the futility of her hope. She was still a prisoner, still in prison. Yes, this apartment was a prison, however luxurious, and it was meant for her.

Then Floretta remembered her flower.

* * * * *

Floretta was still mourning the loss of her flower when she lay down to sleep that night in the large soft bed of her apartment. It grieved her that, after having recovered possession of it for the second time, she had been forced to leave it yet again and then one day exactly ago. It had been in a bedchamber, beside a bed just like the one in which she now lay, but not in this bedchamber, in someone else's, that of the Prince Elbert. And he had been powerless to help her. As her thoughts drifted once more to the Prince, she considered her situation and his, and decided that he could not possibly be as well off as she. For he had not been confined to his apartments, but ripped rudely from them...

When Floretta arose the following morning, she found that more clothes had been laid out for her, and precious jewels placed beside them. The rooms had been tidied, more hot water and clean towels set for her, and fresh flowers arranged in the vases. And in the dining room awaited a fresh meal, equally if not more sumptuous and nourishing, and beside it awaited the faded but still struggling bloom of the iridescent flower!

* * * * *

Floretta spent the whole day joyfully tending her flower, lavishing care on it, coaxing it to greater efforts, offering encouragement, cherishing it. It had fought bravely for its life and now had won; she would not allow anyone to separate her from it again. The flower still maintained its spirit but somehow, it seemed, it had lost its voice…

And so, as more days passed by after the same fashion, and as the flower's voice still did not return, Floretta began to grow lonely. The lovely garden offered her but little consolation; to her it was a gaudy imitation of the loveliness of the forest, a representation of Nature when tamed and 'improved' by human beings. The trees did not speak to her there as they did in the forest. It was as if they were unsure of their role, unsure of their place in the scheme of life.

As for human company, Floretta had none. Her attendants came and went discreetly while she slept; she never succeeded in catching them. And while she knew the guards outside would accost her with words any time she emerged, she did not care to seek out their brusque company.

CHAPTER 28

On the afternoon of the fifth day, a visitor came at last to Floretta. She started upon hearing the door open and, turning, was relieved to see the innocuous figure of Ashvy Parva. In fact, she felt pleased to see him; he had always treated her well and she could hold him only in high regard.

He bowed to her most respectfully. "My Lady," he addressed her. "His Majesty King Julien has requested that I inquire after your well-being. He is most concerned that your every need be satisfied, that your desires receive complete fulfilment. May I inquire whether your lodging has met with your approval?"

"Of course you may inquire and of course my lodging has met with my approval," she told him, her tongue loosened by the impatience of her loneliness but untainted by anger towards him.

"And the articles of clothing," he asked, "and the other presents, are they to your liking?"

"But of course they are to my liking. How could they be otherwise?"

"And the meals which have been prepared, they have proved palatable?"

"But of course, of course!" she replied.

"My Lady sounds impatient," he observed politely. "Can it be that, in our foolishness, we have overlooked some obvious desire? My Lady would perhaps enjoy the distraction of music? I could arrange the attendance of a company of musicians or fools... Or perhaps My Lady would enjoy the company of an affectionate animal? A cat? A dog?"

"You are right," she admitted, "in your observation that I lack company. My every bodily need is catered for in the extreme, but I waste away through enforced solitude!"

"I am much grieved to hear this," he replied, "and must see that the omission is rectified. If it please My Lady, I myself will provide her companionship for a while?"

"It does please me," she told him, "for I long to speak about my condition, and my own ears do not suffice. If I speak to them, they listen, as do the walls, but they provide no answers. I consider my chances, I discuss my future, but evoke no reply. If I spoke to you, would you listen and reply? For you are among the few that I have learned to trust here. But should I speak, for should I trust you?"

"My Lady perceives correctly," he replied, seating himself beside her on her settee, "that it will be my duty to report to my master following my visit here, but she may be assured that in fulfilling my duty, I will exercise the greatest of tact."

"Then tell me," she begged, "dear Parva, please tell me, when might I be freed? For I long so much to go home; it seems I am to be denied naught else."

"Sadly, My Dear Lady," he replied, "I am quite powerless to answer your question, as it is not within the scope of my ability accurately to predict the whim of my king."

"But can you not offer then some hint of why I am being kept here?"

"Alas, My Lady, as to that matter, His Majesty has not yet confided in me and I will not exceed my liberties to speculate... It is however to be expected that, when His Majesty is less troubled by Affairs of State, he will find time to visit you here and express his intentions for you himself. In the meantime, all that I may do to help you is to arrange the satisfaction of any desire."

"But, Parva," she insisted. "You know that all my desires are already satisfied save one: I desire now only my freedom. If you really wish to help me, then tell me what I must do to secure my release. What does His Majesty expect of me? What part must I play in this charade? What magical powers are attributed to me now? Why does he confine me in luxury when I fancied I was to be executed?"

"To all these questions, My Good Lady, I have no answer," he replied. "But I will convey your concern to His Majesty, if such is your wish, that he may reply himself."

"Yes, that is my wish."

"I have but one suggestion myself," Parva told her, "concerning your future. And it is this, that whatsoever His Majesty asks of you, you provide it straightway with no quarrel or protest."

Floretta did not understand. "But what if he again asks of me something which I cannot give?"

"Then," replied Parva, "it might be advisable for you to create some illusion of providing such a service. I might myself be able to advise and assist you in this."

"But such a deception would be quite... dishonourable," she told him. "Do you indeed recommend that I comply with the King's wishes even if this involves me in action... against my better judgement?"

"That is exactly my recommendation," he said. "Whatever may be His Majesty's request, even if it be offensive to your person, I advise that you accord it."

"But, but... why?" she asked.

"My dear!" he insisted. "For your own sake!"

"But," she objected, "that which is done purely for one's own sake is not necessarily good. And I would not wish to act counter to goodness. For is not goodness more important than oneself?"

Parva shook his head in amazement. "What is this 'goodness' of which you speak?" he asked. "Does it exist? Can you define it? I think not."

She was indeed at a loss to provide a definition: to her 'goodness' had always been such a certainty, such an absolute — however distant and intangible — that she had never questioned it. In her search for words, she found herself resorting to the many conversations she had had with her father the forest on the subject. They now granted her little inspiration — she recalled too well the forest's tendency to offer warnings rather than any positive guidance.

"Goodness exists!" she declared with conviction — conviction based more on intuition than on reasoning. "But I cannot tell you what it is, and will not be able to, until such a time as I reach a state of goodness. Neither am I in a position to tell you how to reach that state, though I do continually strive for it."

Parva offered no reply to this but sat listening attentively, and so she decided to expatiate. "There is no simple set of guidelines to be followed," she told him. "If you wish to define goodness, you may well do better to list types of behaviour to be avoided. The conscience will offer guidance here and must be consulted anew with each fresh situation; and, as is relevant to our discussion, the conscience will frequently dictate action counter to the immediate interests of the self."

Parva shook his head again, as if in disbelief. "You must learn," he told her, "to rid yourself of these ideas. They constitute a dangerous state of mind. Reconcile these concepts of goodness and self. There is no dichotomy. To me the two are fused. That which benefits oneself is good. Do not be persuaded by the timorous misgivings of your conscience to think otherwise."

"But," she probed, "do you never experience misgivings — qualms — when following the instructions of the King?" Parva appeared to her a person of integrity: intelligent and self-controlled, thoughtful and considerate. She found it difficult to accept that a person of these apparent qualities could be devoid of conscience.

"No," he replied decisively, though giving himself no time for reflection. "I allow myself no qualms, for, to possess qualms, in that direction lie madness and destitution. It is not for me to doubt decisions but to implement them; my life and livelihood depend on this. I have long since denied myself the luxury of doubt. If I paused to doubt the rectitude of every instruction, it would lead ultimately to the dereliction of my duties and my career would be forfeited."

"Then," she regretted, "you have lost sight of goodness in your career."

"The goodness which you speak of," he replied, "is defunct. And so is anyone who seeks to follow it. It is easy to follow 'goodness' to the grave, though, I admit, martyrdom is no easy folly. I see goodness as that which advances the living. And, in particular, my living. And, inasmuch as His Majesty's advancement will likewise advance my living, my interests ally themselves precisely with his, and goodness becomes that which will satisfy his wishes. Which means I am here not merely through an altruistic desire to warn you but also, at his bidding, in the hope that I may persuade you to do his will."

* * * * *

Parva returned to see Floretta again the following afternoon. Again she was pleased to see him, and again she asked when she might be free, or when she might know what was expected of her, and once more he assured her of his inability to reply.

"But what of His Majesty's decision to execute me?" she asked. "Why does he expend his wealth on me and keep me in every luxury if I am to die? Can you not tell me this?"

"My dear," he replied. "You merely ask the same question but in a different form. I cannot answer 'why?'. But all the same, I had not heard myself that His Majesty had plans to execute you, although you must not doubt for one moment that a threat of death constantly hangs over you. And so you can rest assured that, at the moment, he is not intending to execute you, for if he were, I would have heard a whisper."

"But," she insisted, "when I was captured – in Prince Elbert's bedroom, that is – he assured everyone present that 'naturally' I would have to die as well…"

"No doubt that memory is correct," he replied, "but I would advise you to erase it. Do not imagine that you would benefit from reminding His Majesty of such a remark if he himself has already forgotten it." Parva almost smiled. "Do not complain at an unexpected and unexplained reprieve."

"So at least I will not die," she said. "But what of Prince Elbert? Is he to die? Has sentence been passed upon him, or is he still to be tried? And what of me, will I be required to appear at his trial? It occurs to me now that maybe I am detained here for that purpose."

"If my information is correct," he told her, "His Royal Highness the Prince Elbert has already stood trial. Your presence was obviously considered superfluous."

"How then?" she asked. "What then was the verdict?"

"Why, guilty, of course," replied Parva. "For would he have been taken to trial had there been any doubt?"

"But there was every doubt," declared Floretta. "He had done no wrong."

"The verdict indicated otherwise."

"You say that merely because it was the verdict of your master," she accused, looking Parva straight in the eye.

"Exactly so," he agreed, returning her gaze.

"You feel no misgiving at the condemnation of an innocent man?" she asked.

"No misgiving," he replied. "I allow myself no luxury of misgiving."

"But if you heard the evidence!" she declared. "The charge was fictitious! The evidence was fabricated! All truth was suppressed!"

"I have no desire to hear the evidence," he said. "For do you imagine I could assist the Prince even if I wished? Do you imagine that I could assist you in your predicament now, that is, supposing I decided it would benefit me? I have power only inasmuch as my master grants me it; I have no power to act against him. And so, I have no desire to trouble my conscience with the sordid details of any miscarriage of justice. I ask you to spare me that."

"So then you do have a conscience," Floretta rejoined. She had always suspected as much.

Parva made no reply.

"Is Elbert then to die?" Floretta asked quietly.

"Are you enamoured of him?" asked Parva.

"What?" Floretta was taken aback. "No!" But her denial to Parva was less a denial to herself and more a question, for until then she had not considered the possibility he put before her. And as she began to consider it, she realised that, in part at least, her denial had been a lie, for she was a little, just a very little, in love with Elbert. She understood now why he had haunted her thoughts: she did admire certain facets of his character: he appeared sincere, ingenuous and affectionate, even though in the final moment he had revealed himself to be more lacking in moral fibre than one would perhaps have wished… She remembered having felt unsure as to where right lay in the Royal Household; she now had no difficulty in deciding that, even if it did not lie completely with Elbert, it lay more with him than with Julien.

"I am pleased to hear it," Parva was saying. "I trust you speak the truth for it is better that your emotions are not involved in this affair. As you appear to have no special regard for the Prince Elbert, I will reveal that at present he is still alive."

"Thank goodness," breathed Floretta, and immediately regretted those two revealing words. "How long then will he live?" she asked.

"One cannot say," Parva replied. "As long as it may please the King. One cannot pronounce on such matters with any certainty."

"The Prince is being confined in the dungeons?"

"So it is to be believed."

"Then why does His Majesty recoil from the final step of execution?" asked Floretta. "For he appears to possess no scruples, and is he not intent on removing the threat of Elbert's opposition?"

"His Majesty is not entirely without regard for his cousin," replied Parva. "After all, they grew up together; they were playmates. And, you need understand, the threat of Elbert, as you put it, has already been removed by his conviction and imprisonment. So now His Majesty hesitates, especially as all other opposing elements now seem intent on quitting the country. There will soon be little hint of opposition. In fact, there already is none."

"The Duchess of Ferrar…"

"She has left, and taken her children."

"But leaving her eldest son?"

"She was powerless to help him and knew it. In fact her departure may be seen to have lengthened his life; she herself is wise enough to have realised that. If she had stayed and fought, Elbert would have died. And, knowing what it was to lose one of her dearest persons, she took a gamble and left. Also, no doubt, she wished to ensure she did not lose the third and last man in her life, for it must be admitted that her younger son Rupert showed sufficient spirit soon to have condemned himself."

"And she will not return…" murmured Floretta.

"No," said Parva. "She will not return. For I doubt if she could ever arouse sufficient enmity against our king in neighbouring lands to produce a show of might. She cannot help you… I tell you these things, My Lady, because of my admiration for you, that you will more readily appreciate the completeness and permanence of the situation. I tell you for no other reason. For I would not wish you to condemn yourself with futile opposition to His Majesty's demands."

CHAPTER 29

"Be upstanding for His Majesty the King!" cried Ashvy Parva. The doors had been thrown suddenly open and Floretta had already sprung to her feet.

The King entered, King Julien I, very proud, very regal, very self-assured. He regarded Floretta with a look of interest and yet of disdain; she returned his gaze and on impulse performed a little curtsey, though not as a mark of esteem, more as an act of boldness, to show that she had not been petrified by his magisterial presence.

"You may leave," the King told Parva.

Parva bowed and, to Floretta's deepest regret, departed, leaving herself and the King alone, she to her resources and he to his. She no longer felt so sure of her boldness; she remembered the words of the Duchess of Ferrar: "Think three times before you speak, or he will trap you with your own words!" Would she fare any better than the Prince Elbert?

"I trust my butler has attended your every desire and served you well?" inquired the King.

"Indeed, Your Majesty," she replied. "I can confirm without any reservation that the standard of his service has been most excellent."

"Good," he replied. "Your words please me, for so on my command is it to be. As you must understand, I wish to offer you a life of unparalleled refinement and luxury as befits your beauty and quality. I trust therefore that leisure has agreed with you? Though I fancy that I need not ask, for I can see that it has: your health is much improved, and you are possessed of the beginnings of a grace."

"Your Majesty," she replied. "It is true that this week has allowed me a complete convalescence, and I wish to offer no criticism of Your Majesty's hospitality and generosity, but alas, if I am to be truthful, I must declare that this week I have wasted and pined. For uninterrupted solitude is an unnatural state which does not become me."

"That is most unfortunate." He sounded genuinely regretful: Floretta almost doubted her conviction that he had come for no good. "If My Lady feels that she has in some way been deprived of company, and fancies that I myself may somehow have been instrumental, then I can only express my deepest sorrow. For such was not my intention. But, it must be appreciated, during this the first week of my reign, my duties have been so onerous that I have been allowed very few spare moments for personal matters. It is to be hoped that in the future I will be able to afford My Lady greater attention…"

Floretta refrained from replying; she had no desire for the King's attention but knew better than to tell him so. Instead she curtseyed in acknowledgement of his offer: a neutral gesture.

"I must also arrange," he continued agreeably, "for ladies to be selected, ladies-in-waiting, to provide companionship when I myself cannot be here, companionship in womanly matters as reading or sewing. It is indeed the business of selecting such companions which inspired my presence today, for there are, it goes without saying, many who would desire to serve and yet few who would be worthy. It is of course for My Lady to choose…"

Floretta found this apparent magnanimity almost impressive, but her response was marred by deep-rooted scepticism: how could she ever trust a man who in the past had shown himself in such bad light?

"My thoughts were promoted in this matter," he continued, "by the unexpected arrival of an applicant this very day. The lady asked for you by name and declared she would serve no other. A compliment indeed! I am certain she referred to your person; she called you by name: the Lady Floretta?"

This was a shock. Floretta looked up startled.

"Ah!" he remarked. "Then we were not mistaken."

"Is that lady still here?" asked Floretta, hoping her eagerness did not show. The 'applicant' could only be her mother, of whom she longed for news.

"Alas, no," the King went on. Did she detect a hint of sarcasm in his words? "I myself interviewed her cursorily and then sent her away, for she lacked your grace. I did not imagine you would wish to be served by such a tired, wizened old woman, a woman not so much old as looking old, aged as it were by hard labour or by suffering before her time…"

Floretta was further alarmed. Despite the King's supercilious manner, she believed what he said and suspected no trick; she did not doubt that someone had come asking for her: how else could he have learnt her name? Surely Elbert hadn't told him? But what of his remarks concerning the caller's age? If they were true, then the caller could not have been her mother. But who else could it have been? Her grandmother? She was the only elderly person of Floretta's close acquaintance and the description would fit. But her grandmother's being was submerged beneath that of her mother; she had no separate existence. Or, at least, on their last meeting so had it been…

"The old woman may have been my grandmother," she sighed. "I would indeed have wished to see her…"

"Your grandmother?" he replied mildly. "Your statement surprises me, for I had been assured that of your family you had only your mother."

"The caller will then have been my mother," agreed Floretta artlessly. "For no one outside my family would seek me. And I would equally have wished to see her."

"Your mother?" he pursued. "So you concede then that you have no grandmother? My information was all along correct?"

Abruptly, Floretta realised the foolishness of her remarks. Too late, she saw the trap he had set: he had tricked her into appearing to contradict herself. But for what purpose? She reconsidered his words but, though she realised there was some scheme underlying them, could not discern what it was. She reconsidered her own words: she had played into his hands by chance remarks. And she might do so again: for how could she avoid his devices without knowing his design? She decided that far greater caution was called for – she must not allow herself to be caught off guard again.

"I do have a grandmother," she replied warily, attempting some sort of explanation, "but she was rarely disposed to reveal herself."

"Ah!" he pounced. "And so you assume that the caller was indeed your mother! How so? Has your mother in common with your grandmother the appearance of an old woman?"

"No, My Lord," she stammered. "I, I would not describe her as particularly old."

"What age then is she?"

"Indeed Sir, I know not," she protested. "Her exact years are not known to me; she has never told me and it has never interested me to inquire." Floretta was growing annoyed at the competition in chicanery in which she had become involved; with her annoyance came a resurgence of her boldness: she would be open if he would not. "Equally, Your Majesty," she continued, "I cannot understand why the matter should interest you. I can sense that you require something of me, but I would have imagined that you would desire something rather more than details of my mother's age! Will you not be more frank and reveal truly what you desire?"

"Very well…" he replied slowly. "Though the words do not come easily to me. For I wish of you very much, indeed all that you can give. But in return, I shall give you much more, much much more, all that I can give, all that might ever be given by a king."

"If I can give you anything in the name of goodness, then I will give it," agreed Floretta. "But, Sir, still you fail to answer. You speak in riddles. Speak out, I beseech you, and be plain!"

"Directness eludes me," he replied, "for all that I desire stems from my admiration of your beauty. The strength of my admiration is such that I long to possess your beauty, to possess it and yet still to share it with you."

"Sir, I entreat you, be direct!" she insisted. "Seek not to confound me with high-sounding compliments!"

"You must forgive my reticence," he replied. "For it derives from the involvement of the trickster Elavisado who, we have already agreed – have we not? – is to our mutual misfortune known to us both. The matter is this: he has recently been brought into my custody and, that I might pardon him for his deceptions and misdemeanours, has been attempting to render himself of assistance. Already today he has proved himself useful by identifying the crumpled little old woman who called here begging for a glimpse of you…" He paused.

"Go on," asked Floretta quietly.

"He swore on his life that the haggard old creature could be none other than the woman known until recently as your mother, though he could now recognise her by her mannerisms and features alone. His amazement was extreme, it bordered on fear: you see, for your mother to be that woman she must by necessity have aged ten years, twenty years, even thirty years, in weeks…"

Now that the King appeared at last to be talking openly, Floretta began in spite of herself to cry. Her tears were cold and bitter: the warmth of the love in them, though great, could not defeat the chill of her deep despair. The truth was apparent; she accepted the King's cruel words at face value, though she herself did not imagine her mother had aged. Rather, she visualised the eclipse of her mother's personality in the absence of herself and the flower, an eclipse for which the corresponding re-emergence of her grandmother's faded spirit would only partially compensate. In a short time, neither would have the energy for life.

"And if we were to compare that fresh report with others offered by Elavisado some weeks ago," continued the King relentlessly, "our amazement would exceed even the extreme. For previously described to me was the mystery of a maiden so lovely with a mother so youthful that the two could masquerade as a pair of delightful sisters…"

"I suspect that the visitor was indeed my grandmother," murmured Floretta, no longer fully listening to him.

"I think not," disagreed the King. His tone had become much less pleasant – and more urgent. "You have one kinswoman only, whom I doubt to be your grandmother or even your natural mother. She is more like in truth your sister! I suspect you of age akin to hers, an age far beyond your complexion and young girl's tears, and of a secret which I desire…

"And you cannot deny that you have this secret. You in my care maintain your youth quite unaided and even blossom! While your sister in your absence shrivels and fades and yearns for you to return and deliver her! You and only you are the keeper of the secret, the Secret of Eternal Youth!"

A gasp almost of horror escaped from Floretta's lips as her tears continued to flow.

"We pondered whether to detain the white-haired old witch, your sister, but concluded that she could serve no use – she had no spells – she merely diluted yours, it seemed – and so we sent her away to her hovel. But if you wish her to return – and you did indeed declare that you would wish to see her – that could be arranged. I can allow her the opportunity to recover, to recuperate in a life of sublime luxury equal to your own. I will permit it. You see, oh beautiful one, your tears, if genuine, are quite superfluous. You need not grieve for your decrepit sister…

"I ask merely that you share your secret with me. As your sovereign, I have the right to demand it. I ask no more and in return offer you everything. If you wish to be queen, in time that can be so. And for you the wait will not seem so protracted, for when one is used to immortality, does not a day become as a minute and a year as a day? For the moment, for these few days, I have a queen – the lovely Marianna whom I could not harm – but I would not wish her with me for all eternity. She will not obstruct you. I will be content when her time is spent and she has left me. For must not immortals reconcile themselves to the loss of favourite persons, as a man must reconcile himself to the loss of a pretty pet?

"When these few short days of waiting are past, by then, in the sharing of our proud secret, our love will have grown very strong and you will remain my glad queen forever. Your dreams? Voice them! For I can fulfil them, as you fulfil mine! The share of all my riches, of all my power, is yours! My land, my prestige, my majesty…"

"No," Floretta shook her head and tried to speak up through her tears. "No, no, no! This cannot be!"

"Cannot be? Are you so loath to share your power that you become seized with anger and choke on hot tears at the suggestion? Cannot be? Or will not be?"

"It cannot be!" insisted Floretta. "It is impossible!"

"The choice is yours," he concluded. "I still give you the choice, though you give me none. I present you with two alternatives: the first, immediate tormented death as befits the witch you are known to be, and the second, an eternal and luxurious life." He turned towards the door. "On the morrow I will hear your final decision."

CHAPTER 30

At first Floretta felt devastated by the King's ultimatum, but, having been under threat of execution before, only to find the threat had possessed no substance, she found herself wondering if she had any real cause to feel afraid this time. But he had sworn to return to demand an answer from her and she felt sure he would. And she had no answer to give, none that would satisfy him. From this sense of personal inadequacy, rather than from a belief in the seriousness of the King's threat, stemmed her fear. It seemed impossible to her that he would actually want to kill her, but she fancied that if she did not do as he bid he might feel honour bound to do so.

Floretta voiced her anxiety to the iridescent flower: to the augmentation of her grief it did not reply. She found herself wishing that Ashvy Parva would come: he would offer consolation even if no sound counsel.

He would probably suggest some complicated ruse by which they might seek to deceive the King, but she wanted none of it. Or did she? Was it perhaps the possibility of assistance in such a ruse which prompted her to thoughts of Ashvy Parva? Floretta found this possibility alarming. She searched her conscience.

Maybe, as Parva suggested, she should pretend to possess the desired secret. After all, though she knew herself to lack the aptitude for pretence, the King would eagerly believe her. She and Parva could sustain the make-believe for weeks at least; perhaps even years would go by before the King came to realise that his age had not stood still. But what if he arranged for her grandmother to be brought to the Palace? She would surely not regain her youth again as the King expected. And would not his suspicions then be much sooner aroused? In his anger he would subject Grandmother and not just Floretta to the tormented death he spoke of. The thought of causing suffering to someone so dear caused Floretta herself pain.

She could perhaps succeed in disowning Grandmother and banishing her to the forest. It would be for her own sake. But even that would be cruelty to the old woman: rejected by her treasured Floretta, she would die of a broken heart. And what kind of life could Floretta live without her? What loneliness, what emptiness she would experience, even amid the splendours of the Palace.

Moreover, any pretence to the King could not result in her saving her mother. For her mother, Floretta could see no hope: the spirit of Flora would soon be extinguished forever: it had departed from the body which it had shared with Grandmother, she presumed, yet showed no sign of returning to the muted, insentient flower.

But what of herself? Should Floretta lie to save herself? The King offered to fulfil all her dreams. She could express all her dreams quite quickly and simply, and yet, she knew that if she did, he would not fulfil them. He would never believe the stuff of her dreams, never accept that she wished to relinquish luxury and grandeur for the bareness of a tiny cottage; he would suspect merely that she was scheming to escape from him (and he would be partly right).

Tears came once more to Floretta as she realised quite finally that never, never, never again would she share a humdrum, hard-working and yet happy existence with her mother or her grandmother in their cottage, not even for one day. Her only dream, though simple, lay far beyond the realms of possibility. Not one hour, not even one minute, would she spend with either of her loved ones again.

And lying would not change that. Only in the truth lay hope, and that spark of hope burned very feeble, very small. But hope there was. If she spoke boldly to the King and assured him again that she had no secret, that the miracles that had frequented her family had not been her doing... Would he believe her? Could he understand? The chance was only small, but to Floretta it appeared her only chance. She had rejected scheming or deceit.

* * * * *

"And so I conclude that my mother must once more be dead," Floretta explained sadly to the King. "As the flower withered following its separation from us, so did my mother's spirit begin to wither in its absence. And even though the flower has somewhat revived, it is not as before, and I see that my mother's spirit has not been received back into it. The flower has lost its sentience."

"But," King Julien objected. "If the presence of the flower sustained your mother's life, why then was it unable to sustain my father's?"

"I do not fully understand these things," Floretta replied, "but I imagine that the flower was incapable without me. Without me, it had already withered." It was only a suggestion.

"It is just as I thought. Again we return to the conclusion of your supreme power."

"No," she insisted. "For even though the flower is helpless without me, I can achieve nothing without it."

"Then why did you not save my father when you and your flower were united? I lose patience with your lies. I begin even to suspect that you desired my father's death."

"No, My Lord," sighed Floretta. "You cannot accuse me of this. I bore your father no ill, and you know it. He died because he had reached the end of his days. It is sometimes too late to save a life. Just as it was too late for me to save the flower."

"But you have saved the flower. You have it here with you now and its health is perfect. In fact its incredible recovery is merely a further sign of your power."

"No, no," she answered. "Do you not understand? I have told you, its power is gone. It blooms, yes, its colours glow one more, but its magic has left it and will never return."

"This I do not accept."

"But My Lord," she insisted. "Even if the flower had flourished at your father's bedside, I suspect it could not have saved him. It is the medium only of my mother's life. It could not transmit life to any other. It is not a charm for youth."

"You do not convince me."

"How can you doubt my sincerity," she implored. "You have lost your father and it troubles you, but remember, I too have lost my dearest one. Would I have allowed this to happen if I really did possess wondrous powers?"

"You employ the same false argument. You refer to mother and grandmother and claim to mourn the loss of one, whilst admitting that the two are one! You have lost nobody. Your mourning is a device which you have constructed to extricate yourself from my grasp. You wish to escape me so that you may concentrate your powers on renewing the youth of your kinswoman."

"No, My Lord. I wish merely the freedom to care for my grandmother in her last months."

"Enough! I will not allow you to go forth and monopolise your talents. I insist, as sovereign of this land and as owner of all I see, that you share your bounty with me!"

"I have nothing to share with you."

"I do not doubt your reluctance, just as I do not doubt the falsity of your tales. Your story is appealing but quite absurd. I now tire of it. I will take my leave of you and, in doing so, I remind you once more of the choice before you: immediate tormented death as befits the witch who allowed my father to die, or an eternal and luxurious life. Your decision will be heard tomorrow."

CHAPTER 31

Once more a stay of sentence; no progress at all had been made. Floretta felt herself weary and then angry at the delusions and obduracy of this man who was king. He had placed her in a seemingly eternal purgatory, with no escape to any other place. It appeared that he would never actually kill her, but merely continue his threats, while on the other hand he would never free her. Grandmother would need to die alone. Here in the apartment that was her prison, Floretta was powerless to assist her.

It seemed that the only valuable service to humankind which she might possibly perform in her present situation would be to present the King with the many truths which his own servants apparently shrank from sharing with him. She did not blame them for their moral cowardice before so suspicious and so mighty a master, but resolved that she herself would not be afraid to speak.

The morrow came and passed slowly, each long moment spent in expectation of the sudden arrival of the King. Night fell and still he had not come. Floretta continued waiting for him until late in the evening. At length she retired, but her troubled sleep provided little release from the tension of her day, and she was glad when the light of another day greeted her, even though she knew it would bring merely the agony of further waiting.

In the afternoon, at last, Floretta was summoned from her apartment. She felt almost relieved: she suspected danger but was glad for an end to the waiting. Sensing the possibility that she might not return and not wishing to repeat her error of previous occasions, Floretta took along the flower.

She was escorted by guards through the labyrinth of echoing corridors to a chamber whose paucity of furnishings added to its impression of great size. The doors closed upon her as the guards withdrew, leaving her quite alone, it seemed, so that she could only guess as to why she had been brought to this hall.

The rich dark panelling of the walls and ceiling gave a mellow effect, and yet the room was not dim: the many tall windows along one long wall allowed in the sun of the warm afternoon so that the bright rays reflected cheerfully upwards from the gleaming highly polished ebonite surface of the floor. The windows looked out across the Palace courtyard to the market place. Floretta could see that it was market day: she longed to be away from the Palace, out there among the common folk, participating in the noise and bustle, the barest murmur of which reached her in this cool room. Sadly, Floretta averted her eyes from the tantalising view and considered instead the strange room where she stood.

Despite the lack of carpeting and of comfortable furnishings the room was not bare: a blazonry of heraldic shields and banners and of antiquated weapons adorned the walls. Dominating the display was the collection of richly jewelled regalia: gloriously decorated golden monstrances, each bearing the name of the great personage whose remains it purported to contain; beside these, sceptres, chalices, an orb, a sword, and then the royal crowns, all encrusted with bright gems of every hue. And beyond the display from where Floretta stood, central to the long wall facing the windows, there were two thrones, one very grand and elaborate, the other less so but still very fine.

As the thrones caught Floretta's eye, she realised with a start that the larger was occupied: she could see merely the hands, knees and feet of the occupant. At that moment a voice issued suddenly from the throne: "Well, witch?" it demanded. The voice resounded about the empty chamber but the speaker did not reveal himself. "May I have your decision, or are you still prevaricating? Do you wish to sit here beside me as my queen or shall I cast you before the callous mob for their ruling upon your fate? If you so wish, I could demand their attention this very minute that you might throw yourself upon their meagre mercy. Or do you not wish that? You must hurry and choose. Choose! The choice, you have surely realised, is between eternal heaven and eternal hell." He paused. "I myself am already in heaven; if you will make my heaven eternal then you may join me in it, but if you seek to thwart me then you will be damned!"

Floretta was unabashed by the King's manner; she merely felt rather annoyed by his tiresome arrogance. In no way had her resolve to speak plainly been quashed.

"You yourself will be damned," she declared, moving across the room so that she faced him. "If we are to believe in damnation, that is. For your obsession with grandeur, your pretensions to deity."

He merely laughed. "Strange words indeed from a witch!" he mocked. "And how strange a witch she is! It appears she feels able to escape damnation! Methinks it is by her damnation of me that she hopes to achieve her own apotheosis!"

"Indeed, no, Sir," she replied calmly. "I criticise you through no motive of personal gain, merely in the pursuit of truth. For I feel no threat of damnation: I am no witch. Unless, that is, it is possible for me to have become one without my intent or knowledge."

For some moments the King appeared unable to phrase a reply. "How amusing," he remarked at length, "that an upstart such as yourself should feel above criticism whilst criticising a king upon his throne. But it is no wonder that you feel no fear in my presence, I realise now, no wonder that you dare to criticise and provoke me: you, who see yourself as immortal, as above death or damnation, and quite justifiably, I suppose. But I, in my earthly power, will curtail your confident expectations. I will crush you, quarter you, dissect you, destroy every ounce of your physical entity, and reduce you once more to the petty status of mortality."

"I am content with my mortality," replied Floretta. "Would that you could better reconcile yourself to yours."

"Ho, ho!" he answered almost gleefully. "So you will gladly meet your death? Well, we shall soon see... As for myself, my death is very far off. It is not for a king as youthful as myself to waste his energies considering so remote a possibility."

"Death is not a remote possibility," she told him soberly, "nor even a remote probability, but one of the definite promises of time. And a promise which is never quite so remote that one should neglect to prepare for it."

"You speak now as one who knows death may well be imminent," he replied. "I am not in that position. It is absurd that I should prepare myself for my own demise, unless, that is, you scheme at this very moment to procure it. Perhaps I have uncovered your design? I advise you against this: it would merely confirm your own untimely end."

"I am powerless to cause Your Majesty's death," she told him, "and anyway would not wish to do so, so do not attribute me that crime too. As always you deny truth and replace it with fiction. I am as unable to procure your death as I would be to postpone it."

"Oh, well," he replied casually. "If I must accept that it is so, if you really are unable to assist me in the prolongation of my youth as I had hoped, then you are of no further use to me, and I may as well rid myself of the burden of you and dispose of you forthwith."

"You imply that you are prepared to execute yet another innocent person," she replied daringly, yet with a detachment and calm equal to his. "And this time not even through political necessity but merely to satisfy a personal whim."

Surprisingly to Floretta, the King appeared annoyed; she had perhaps touched his pride – or a raw nerve. "And who, by your reckoning," he demanded, "have I executed for political reasons?"

Floretta hesitated; it would serve no purpose to provoke his anger. "Possibly more persons than I know of," she replied at length, "though I hope not. One death for which I suspect you are responsible occurred some many days ago now, I believe in this very chamber…"

"Ah!" he answered. "No doubt you refer to the death of my Uncle Ferrar! I deny all association! But what basis can you have for such an accusation? Were you there as witness? Did I myself level the weapon?"

"No… He did not die by your hand but it is possible that it was by your arrangement."

"How so?" he demanded. "We know that his death served my purpose, but can that make me responsible? And then, by popular agreement, my uncle the Duke met with a just end, so are then the people responsible? What tricks of logic you engage in!"

"No," she reminded him. "You express your ideas, not mine; they are your tricks of logic."

He ignored her. "My uncle was assassinated by a loyal subject, who on his apprehension did declare boldly that his only motive was to undo my uncle's unlawful and obscene seizure of power."

Floretta was surprised at the King's willingness to discuss the matter with her; a man in his position had no need to lower himself by protesting innocence or by offering excuses: she was after all quite powerless to condemn him, whatever her opinion of him might be. It did occur to her however that he would surely not speak quite so readily if his conscience were clear. Nonetheless, she could see no reason for him to speak out if he were guilty. She wondered if perhaps he desired to improve his reputation in her eyes, to exonerate himself in some way. How empty this made all his threats seem.

"So you have arrested someone," she said. "I did not doubt you would find a scapegoat to display before the people and to suffer execution on your behalf."

"Oh, no. I have pardoned him," he declared. "How could I punish such loyalty?"

"And the good Colonel Llorens," she asked. "Have you punished him for his loyalty?"

He seemed embarrassed at her mention of the matter. "Llorens has long since been freed," he answered impatiently.

"So you free the men you wrongly accuse," she commented. "But what of your cousin, have you also freed him?"

"There is of course no pardon for my cousin's misdemeanours."

This was so risible that in different circumstances Floretta might have laughed. "But you seek yourself to duplicate them!" she reminded him. "You imprison him because he solicits my company in his apartments but you would, it seems, make me your queen and take me to your own!"

"Perhaps so," he conceded surprisingly. "But he was not king. I am the King and the final judge. And I judged him as he would have judged me, had he been able, though no doubt differently from how he would have judged himself. Likewise I am at liberty to judge myself differently from how he would: I am not subject to his opinion, nor anyone's; as king I am at liberty to act as I wish. In fact, as king it is my duty to do so, for only then can I be sure that I perform my supreme function."

Floretta blinked at this sophistry. "Even though you are king, my judgement of you cannot be as your own," she replied with a sigh.

"But you are not here to sit in judgement over me," he told her peevishly. "It is for me to judge you. And how should I do that? Once again 'differently'? By your conviction instead of mine? Should I decide that the wild witch who throws insults at me is really an angel to be pardoned?"

Floretta did not reply. She was beginning to doubt whether anything constructive had been achieved by her frankness. It seemed that however she chose her words, she could never succeed in bringing this king to view himself in a truer or different light; he listened only as he wished and she could not make him respond reasonably to any sensible point made. She felt their discussion had begun to degenerate.

"I have tired of this charade," he told her. "Let us think instead on sweet things. I can suffer insults from you because the beauty of your anger delights me, but do not test my patience too far. Let us, on your word, return to my apartments and make our peace."

"I have no wish to accompany you to your apartments."

He sighed. "Will you ever play the unapproachable?" he asked. "Perhaps you still doubt my promises? I have told you, and you have heard me, and I mean it as much as ever before, that I would give you anything you might wish."

"I know only," she replied sadly, "that you would never give me anything that I would truly wish."

"Then," he said, "I understand not your wishes."

"It is so."

"How then," he asked, "can I tempt you? For I must have what you alone can offer."

"There is no way."

"So you will not be encouraged by kindness. Likewise you show little response of fear." He paused and, before speaking again, scrutinised her for some moments as if carefully weighing his next move. "But I see," he resumed, still addressing her in a relatively pleasant tone of voice, "I see you have your flower there with you. I have been admiring it. How dear it is to you. Supposing I were to crush it, would you flinch?"

Floretta made no attempt to reply. She had no wish to confirm her great love for the flower to someone she trusted so little, and feared instantly that the rising colour of her hot cheeks would betray her. As she worked hard to repress all sign of emotion from her face, she could sense her efforts would be in vain.

"And would you," he continued, his manner turned quickly cold, "begin within days to turn from a delicious maiden into a repulsive hag? Shall I try it?"

He arose from his throne and descended the steps and began slowly to approach her.

"How foolish," she remarked quickly, stepping back, "to destroy what you believe to be a powerful talisman."

He nodded. "Yes, it would be foolish of you to allow me to do that." He moved slowly towards her. "Why do you retreat from me?" he asked. "Does my form repulse you so much? How surprising then that I do not repulse the lovely Marianna! No doubt I should be thankful. A king can expect the love of only one woman, it seems, though a prince can expect the love of two."

Floretta retreated further. "Then it seems you must become a prince again," she replied, merely to keep him at bay.

"I refer not to myself," he told her icily, "but to my cousin. It seems he has entranced both my sister and my witch!"

"Once more you distort the truth," she replied warily, not wishing to compromise Elbert further by declaring her affection for him, nor yet to deny it. "He has received no encouragement from me."

"No? How then did you persuade him to recover for you your precious flower?" On these words Julien had lashed out and, with one stroke of the hand, had cast the flower from Floretta's grasp. It span across the room until its pot shattered against the hard metal of an ancient sword.

CHAPTER 32

Floretta rushed instinctively to search among the broken shards for the flower, and in the same instant the King rushed at her.

"Leave it!" he cried furiously, dragging her back roughly. "Forget your accursed weed!"

As she struggled to release herself from his grasp and as he grappled with her, he yelled for assistance: "Guards! Guards!"

The doors flew open instantly.

"Seize this girl!" he ordered. "And hold her here!" As his men took Floretta in their iron grip, he backed off at once. Clearly flustered, he brushed himself down and then assumed full voice once more: "And I require the assistance of my butler!"

Ashvy Parva appeared as if by magic. "Your Majesty?" he inquired, as always bowing low.

"This mess must be cleared away immediately," the King told him breathlessly, indicating the fragments of pot and the soil scattered round about. The pieces of plant he now set about gathering himself.

Parva eyed his grovelling master. "Certainly, Your Majesty, will that be all?" he asked.

The King resumed an upright posture. "No, Parva," he told him. "What is more important, I wish you to summon the Palace Herald with all possible haste that he may obtain the attention of the crowd. I now withdraw to prepare myself, but when I return shortly, I intend to address my people." With these words he strode proudly from the room, followed by Parva, leaving Floretta in the custody of the guards.

Parva returned almost at once, bringing with him two housemaids who quickly set about sweeping up the unsightly remains of what had until a few minutes earlier been a lovely thing. Our king destroys beauty, lamented Floretta to herself, because he does not understand it…

"There is no need to restrain the girl so zealously," Parva informed the guards, having apparently noticed the tears in Floretta's eyes. "She cannot run away."

Their grip relaxed but this brought Floretta little relief; she had until then not noticed the tightness of it, her concern and tears having been for the mutilated flower, the mangled remains of which had now departed with the King.

To Floretta Parva hissed: "When will you learn? Time is running short. I have told you, you must submit. There is no other choice. No one can help you, least of all myself. He is quite determined in his threats, I assure you, and is about to offer you up to the people! I warn you: he will ask for your decision no more than three times!"

"I must ask you not to address our prisoner," declared one of the guards.

"Oh, be silent, man!" answered Parva. "Who do you presume you are? Make sure you take good care of this girl!" On these words he stalked out, taking the housemaids with him.

The grip on Floretta's arms at once tightened viciously, so that her eyes began to swim with the pain and so that she scarcely noticed the group of men who entered next. Then trumpets sounded loudly on the balcony and it became clear who the newcomers might be.

"Be silent and attentive for the word of His Majesty the King!" rang out the full, sonorous voice of the Herald. "His Majesty King Julien wishes to address his loyal subjects today on a matter of extreme urgency. You are to be assembled upon the termination of the day's commerce at the hour of four precisely, whereupon His Majesty will appear. Thus spake His Majesty and thus will it be and herewith ends the royal proclamation!"

The hour, it seemed, was close, for very soon Julien had returned and had seized Floretta from the harsh grip of the guards with a grip even more brutal. She tripped over and he half dragged her across the room even though, had he allowed her the opportunity, she would have come of her own volition. He hauled her through the glass doorway out onto the balcony, the same balcony where the Duke of Ferrar had been killed. Floretta saw that his blood still stained the stone. And she saw to her horror that a gigantic unruly crowd had gathered which not only thronged the market place but had also surged into the Palace courtyard to clamour beneath the balcony where she stood.

Julien raised one hand, the other holding Floretta, and the noise of the crowd gradually subsided. "Here is the witch I have promised you!" declared Julien, and the crowd cheered.

He raised his hand again. "This is undoubtedly the witch with whom the Duke of Ferrar and his misguided son plotted my father's death! It is extremely fortunate that we have succeeded in capturing her before she could perpetrate any further evils! You will be pleased to hear that we now have in our custody all the villains! You need no longer live in fear!..

"I summon you here now that you may decide the just retribution for this witch. You may feel that to show mercy and merely to incarcerate her like my ill-starred cousin might grant her scope for further spells. The kingdom must be protected: and I refer here not merely to the Royal Household but more especially to its loyal people."

When the cheering had once more subsided, Julien asked the crowd: "Tell me now, should the witch live or die?"

"Die, die, a witch must die!" shouted the people.

"Die? But how? What manner of death?" demanded the King amid the cries.

"Burn, burn, a witch must burn!" the people began to chant.

The King raised his hand. "When? You must tell me when!" he cried.

"Today, today. She must burn today!" they screamed. "Today, today. Before the day is out!"

"You are wise!" applauded the King. "For we know not what opportunities the mysteries of the dark night might provide her! The burning will then be at sunset and will take place in the market square so that all may witness it!"

The people cheered and cheered, and to Floretta, as her dizzy mind reeled, their cheering appeared to have no end. She had fainted.

"At last I have succeeded in frightening you," the King was saying as her consciousness returned, and he was speaking now more tenderly than triumphantly. "You have one last chance to redeem yourself or you burn this eve. For the third and last time, I ask you to choose between a luxurious life and an unpleasant death."

"You cannot save me, for you have promised the people," she murmured.

"No, no," he insisted. "Do not doubt that the chance to live is open to you. If I can gain from your life, then I will arrange it."

"Then you have deceived your people."

"Not greatly. It is not the majority of the people that have called for your death, merely the roughest and most raucous element. And they can be appeased. We can come to some arrangement. It would be easy enough to satisfy the crowd, simple to obtain another girl in your stead."

The thought of causing an innocent girl as herself such a senseless and horribly painful death merely to save her own life brought the very sensation of that pain to Floretta, so that once more her head swam and again she lost consciousness.

She became gradually aware that her face was being bathed with a cool and soothing lotion. She opened her eyes to find a kindly face looking into hers. She recognised the royal physician, Karezza Avicenna.

"You know I am not a witch," whispered Floretta. "You know that I neither wished nor caused the old King's death. And you know that it was Julien himself that had me brought here."

"My dear young lady," Avicenna replied sadly as he wiped her brow. "How can it be said that I have any knowledge of these matters? Indeed I have none."

But Floretta could see in his troubled eyes that he knew all there was to know.

"Then," she sighed. "No one will save me. I must die at sunset."

EPILOGUE

The crowd were a little disappointed that there were no screams for them to hear, for only rarely did they experience the burning of a witch; none knew that the good physician had drugged the girl. But the people were not dismayed; the spectacle was exciting enough, the tall flames licking the darkening sky.

Among the festive crowd who watched the beautiful girl burn was one who did not share in their rejoicing. This woman was neither old nor young. She looked very tired. It seemed that she wasn't so much old as looking old, aged as it were by hard labour or suffering before her time. It would require exaggeration to describe her as a crumpled or shrivelled or faded, and she was certainly neither wizened, haggard nor decrepit: only a very liberal imagination could have described her so. Her back was not curved but her complexion was wrinkled and freckled now as with someone entering middle age. Only her hair was that of an old woman: her hair was the purest of silver.

Her hair caught the red lights of the flames, as might the bark of the delicate silver birch during a cruel forest fire. Her hair and her eyes blazed with a strong anger, hotter and brighter even than the flames of the fire. In no other way could her anger be seen: she neither moaned nor yelled nor screamed. None of the crowd paused from their enjoyment to question her passivity.

Little more than a week earlier, her hair had been a rich red-gold, as bright as the hair of the beautiful burning girl whose lovely tresses which had gleamed like sunlight were now lost to the envious flames. That hair had been the colour of autumnal gold.

Autumn was coming soon; each day, evening arrived earlier; summer was almost gone. Soon Flora would see the colour of her beloved daughter's hair on the heads of the trees, misty and damp with the tears of autumn. Then even that one small consolation would be taken from her and she would have to endure the harshness and bleakness of a shrill winter with nothing to remind her of her loved one...

But some day, some day, she had faith, spring would come and then, if she ventured into the forest once more, she would at last rediscover her beloved. She would feel the eyes of Floretta opening upon her from all directions, as bank upon bank of wild bluebells re-awoke to the awakening sun. The tender blue-green buds would whisper her name, in unison with the fresh green leaves of the trees, and when the little birds had all returned they too would add their harmony.

Dear Floretta was lost to the World of Man, but she would not be lost to Flora. Floretta was a child of the forest. The life of the human race was bounded by time but not the life of the forest, nor the life of one of its children. Floretta had carried with her the essence of the forest and now that she was leaving the World of Man she would return to the forest and the forest would bear her essence forever.

When the flames of the sunset had long since died away and the flames of the pyre had at last cooled, Flora gathered the charred body of her child from among the ashes and placed it in her apron. She bore it deep into the forest, unafraid of the blackness of the forest night, until she arrived at a secret place where she knew the little body would rest undisturbed. She buried the cherished remains by the inconstant light of the moon, in a little mossy dip with room just for one hidden away behind some rocks and beneath the exposed roots of an old oak. When dawn began to break she returned to her cottage, her courageous heart fighting the sadness which sought to attack it, her shaken spirit encouraged by the promise of spring.

- End of volume one -